DATE DUE		
JAN 2 3		
MAY 0 5 2006		
FEB 2 8		
FEB 1 6 2016		

Cherokee Sister

Cherokee Sister

DEBBIE DADEY

Delacorte Press

Published by
Delacorte Press
an imprint of Random House Children's Books
1540 Broadway
New York, New York 10036

Library of Congress Cataloging-in-Publication Data
Dadey, Debbie.
    Cherokee sister / Debbie Dadey.
        p.   cm.
    Summary: Because she is mistaken for an Indian, twelve-year-old Allie, a white girl, is forced to travel the Trail of Tears along with her best friend, a young Cherokee.
    ISBN 0-385-32703-X
    1. Trail of Tears, 1838 Juvenile fiction. 2. Cherokee Indians Juvenile fiction. [1. Trail of Tears, 1838 Fiction. 2. Cherokee Indians Fiction. 3. Indians of North America—Southern States Fiction. 4. Best friends Fiction. 5. Mistaken identity Fiction.]
    I. Title.
PZ7.D128Ch 2000
[Fic]—dc21   99-23048
                                                                                              CIP

The text of this book is set in 11.5-point Sabon.
Book design by Trish Parcell Watts
Manufactured in the United States of America
April 2000
10 9 8 7 6 5 4 3 2 1
BVG

Cherokee Sister

1

The Beginning

Honeysuckle always reminds me of Leaf and Elisi and long-ago days when the world was different. I was just a scrawny twelve-year-old girl in 1838, but I learned how life can change in an instant and never be the same again. That was the autumn my best friend, Leaf, lost just about everything.

It started on one of those hot, sticky days when I wanted to jump naked into the water and stay there all afternoon. Mama and I had churned butter, collected eggs, weeded the garden, baked bread, and snapped beans the whole morning. When Mama finally took a nap, I grabbed my chance and ran. Most folks would probably think I was ornery taking off like that with Mama getting ready to have a baby and all. Mama had trouble carrying babies and Papa had told me to be sure to help her. I planned on being back before Mama even woke up.

Hopefully, in a few weeks I'd have a baby sister. Or if Papa had his way, a baby brother, so there'd be someone to help him in the fields. I think Mama wanted a boy, too. I would have helped in the fields, but Mama said that was men's work. She said there was plenty to keep me busy around the cabin.

Mostly we just wanted a healthy baby. I said a quick prayer that we wouldn't have to add another little cross to the four already in the family graveyard out beyond the barn and the outhouse.

I ran all the way through the woods, close to the river, and headed for my favorite spot. My friend Leaf Sweetwater and I tried to meet there every day after our morning chores were done. Sometimes she couldn't make it and sometimes I couldn't. But that day Leaf was there, waiting for me on the huge piece of granite we considered our special, private place.

"*Tsi-lu-gi,* Frog-girl," Leaf said, smiling. *Tsi-lu-gi* meant hello in Cherokee. It was one of the few words I knew in her language. Frog-girl was one of the many silly names she had for me. Leaf called me that because the first time we sat at our secret place, a frog had jumped right in my lap and scared me. Leaf hardly ever called me by my real name, Allie.

2

I tried to think of a funny name for her, but I wasn't as clever as Leaf. *"Tsi-lu-gi,* Rock-girl," I said, proud of myself for coming up with something.

"If we were both snow girls, we wouldn't be so hot," Leaf said, making a funny face as if she were frozen.

"If we didn't have to work so much, we could spend all our time in the shade," I said, laughing and brushing sweat from my forehead. "Mama worked me hard all morning. I'm tuckered out." Leaf scooted a basket of leaves and roots out of my way and I plopped down next to her.

"I have looked for medicine plants since sunup," she told me. "Now I am ready to rest." She slipped off her moccasins and laid them beside her basket.

"Me too!" Quickly I unlaced my heavy brown shoes. Off they came, along with my long woolen socks. I laughed and wiggled my sweaty toes. "Ahh! Freedom!" Ever since I turned twelve a few months ago, Mama made me wear shoes, even in the summer. Even when it was so hot I thought my toes would fall off. She said a lady shouldn't be seen without her shoes. I tried to tell her I wasn't a lady. I was just a farm girl, and most farm children didn't wear shoes until the first frost. But Mama insisted and I wore shoes. Leaf probably wore her moccasins just so I wouldn't feel bad. I knew she'd rather be barefoot. Elisi, her grandmother, never cared if Leaf didn't wear shoes. Elisi often went barefoot too.

Our granite rock was a real treasure. It was taller than me, but not as tall as my papa. One side looked like

Mama's belly, filled with a baby, only twenty times bigger. The rock curved over a big hump at the top and the other side was slanted and flat. The slanted side made a perfect resting place, hidden from the path. Leaf and I left our pile of shoes and leaves on the belly and stretched out on the flat side of our secret place. I pulled up my long skirt so my legs could soak up the coolness of the stone. Leaf's brown legs were already bare. We lay on the rock with our heads together. Above us red, orange, and yellow leaves swayed in the slight breeze. A mockingbird sang from a tree branch.

This was my favorite place, hidden away from our tiny cabin and all the work that went along with it. Here I could breathe the sweet honeysuckle and have a place to stretch. Mama wasn't around to scold me for being lazy. On our rock I could dream about never chopping another weed in our garden. I could imagine what it would be like to taste fresh butter and never have to pump the churn myself. I sighed with contentment.

Leaf's eyes sparkled as she leaned toward me. "Elisi finished the dress she's making for me. It has hundreds of tiny blue beads," she said. "It's taken her all season to make it."

Blue was Leaf's favorite color because she loved the sky and birds so much. "You're lucky to have a grandmother like Elisi," I said. "I haven't seen either of my grandmothers since we moved from South Carolina. It's been so long, I don't even remember what they looked like."

"If your grandmothers were here, you'd have a different dress for every day of the week," Leaf told me.

We giggled. I didn't mind that I had only one old dress. After all, Mama had only two dresses. One she kept for Sunday services and one for everyday. But it was fun to pretend that I had more clothes than I could possibly need. "I'd have a white dress for Sunday," I said, twisting a strand of long brown hair around my finger.

"And you'd have a yellow one with a white apron for Monday," Leaf said.

I smiled and closed my eyes. "I'll take a green one for—"

"Did you see that?" Leaf asked suddenly.

"What?" I followed her finger pointing up to the sky. A big bird hung over an opening in the trees. It hovered there for a moment, almost as if it were looking at us. Then it flew away.

"An eagle!" Leaf called. "Something important is going to happen. The eagle was telling us."

I sat up. Leaf believed that things in the woods gave her signs or warnings. I didn't much cotton to any of it. What would happen would happen, and a bird couldn't know anything about it. Sometimes Leaf would get angry at me if I disagreed with her, though. So I held my tongue about the eagle. "My stomach is telling me it's hungry." I changed the subject and stood up. "Let's go down the path for some blackberries. Then we can jump into the river to cool off."

"No," Leaf said firmly. "Just wait. Maybe the eagle will come back."

I sighed and lay back down. Sometimes Leaf could be so stubborn. The day got hotter. Sweat trickled off my face. Nearby a brown squirrel skittered up the peeling bark of a birch tree. In the distance a woodpecker knocked out a beat. After about five minutes I scratched my arm and said, "Come on. It's not coming back."

Leaf held up her hand and whispered, "Listen."

I listened but heard nothing. The mockingbird didn't sing and the woodpecker was still. The sky was bare, without a sign of the eagle. "I don't hear anything," I told Leaf.

She hushed me. "Sometimes nothing means something."

I listened again. Then I figured it out. The silence of the woods was telling us people were near. Quietly I peered over the rock.

Riders emerged on the path not more than a stone's throw from our boulder. A heavy man rode a bay horse and a tall man sat on a black mule. Both had rifles jutting from their saddles. I'd seen the big man on my last trip to town. He wore a sweaty gray shirt, and his horse plodded along under his bulk. I felt sorry for the horse.

The big man spat tobacco juice against a tree and cursed to the other man. "I tell you, Myers, we oughta hunt down every damn Indian and string 'em all up.

Those red demons think they're fit to live among us and marry decent white folks. There's no way one of them will marry my sister."

I ducked and looked at Leaf, a full-blooded Cherokee. She lay perfectly still, but her face was red with anger. When Leaf was angry, she sometimes acted without thinking. I put my hand over her mouth and held it tight. If that fat man saw Leaf he might decide to do a little Indian hunting. I had never been so afraid. I wished we hadn't come to our rock that day. Even though it was hot, gooseflesh sprang up all over my arms and my sweat turned cold. I hated for Leaf to hear the men's awful words. But Leaf acted as if she hadn't heard. She didn't even seem to notice my hand over her mouth. She kept looking at the sky.

If the men saw us, who knew what they would do? At least we were hidden on this side of the boulder. But our shoes! They were on the other side of the rock. What if the men saw Leaf's moccasins? What if they decided to find their owner?

I held my breath. My heart beat so strongly I thought the men might hear it.

"Don't worry, Brownie," Myers bellowed, "the army's gonna take care of the whole mess of 'em soon enough." Even on his little mule, he was much taller than Brownie.

"If it was up to me, I'd shoot 'em all right now," Brownie said with delight.

7

"Blasted heathens shoulda been gone years ago," Myers agreed. "It's the law."

Finally their voices faded away. Peeking over the rock, I saw the dust left by their animals. I scrambled over and grabbed both pairs of shoes, clutching them to my chest.

Leaf kept looking at the sky. "I don't think the eagle will come back today," she whispered. "Maybe we'd better go to my house."

I wanted to tell her I was sorry the men had said those awful things. I wanted to ask if she knew anything about the army. But I didn't get the chance. Leaf snatched her basket and ran. I followed her. I should have gone home, but I felt funny leaving Leaf alone with those crazy white men loose in the forest. She'd be safer if we bumped into them together. And besides, Mama would still be sleeping. She wouldn't even miss me.

2

Leaf's House

By the time we got to Leaf's house my insides were about to burst. "Did you have to run the whole way?" I panted and dropped the moccasins and shoes in a pile beside the well before sitting down.

"Here, this will make you feel better." Leaf lowered the bucket into the well and pulled out fresh water. She offered me a drink from a blue metal dipper. "Have some *ama*."

"*A-ma*," I said slowly. Leaf and her older brother, Cobb, were always trying to teach me new Cherokee words. I was eager to learn but pitifully poor at remembering them later. I sipped the water and tried hard to put the Cherokee word in my brain. "Ahhh, that tastes so good! I could take a bath in this."

"All right!" Leaf smiled and dumped the rest of the cold water on my head.

"Ohhhh! What'd you do that for?" I sputtered and jumped to my feet.

Leaf giggled. "You said you wanted to take a bath, Fish-girl."

I grabbed the bucket away from her and wiped the water from my face. "You know I didn't mean it." I searched for a word to call her. "Have some water yourself, Water-bucket-girl." I was all set to give Leaf a soaking when I kicked her moccasin with my foot and my good spirits disappeared. I was so grateful the men hadn't seen the moccasins. I couldn't easily forget the men's hateful words. My stomach still churned with fear for Leaf.

"Do you think those men meant it when they said they wanted to kill Indians?" I hated to say it out loud, but I was plenty worried about Leaf.

"Town folk always talk that way," Leaf said as she took the bucket and hung it on its peg. "I've heard them when they're riding by on the trail."

I had heard people grumble about Indians too, when I went to town with Pa. But they never scared me like those men. This talk was meaner. With Leaf beside me, it had seemed so real. "Do you know what the army is up to?" I asked.

10

"No. Probably just some more white people hating Cherokees," she said. "There's nothing new about that. Come on in, let's get something to eat."

Leaf lived in a two-story log building set in a dusty clearing. A big, wide porch ran along the whole front of the house, which was both Leaf's home and a trading post. The top floor contained three little bedrooms, one each for Leaf, her grandmother, and Leaf's older brother, Cobb. Leaf's parents and grandfather had died long before from the measles. Leaf was lucky her grandmother was so good at business. I had never known anyone who had a bigger house or nicer things than Leaf.

The big trading post room took up most of the first floor. There was also a tiny storeroom, and a good-sized keeping room, where Leaf's family took their meals. I never got used to how big Leaf's house was. We had only two rooms: the keeping room or main room, where I slept, and Mama and Papa's small bedroom. Our house might not be as fancy as Leaf's, but it was warm and safe.

Leaf's grandmother ran the trading post with her grandson, Cobb. There wasn't another store within a day's ride, so lots of people used it. If they didn't go to Sweetwater's they'd have to go the whole way into town—a day's ride one way—just to get supplies.

Leaf's grandfather had built the business through hard work when Leaf's grandmother was even younger than my mama. When her husband died, Elisi took over the store. She worked just as hard as her husband. People trusted and liked her. She always had kind words for those she traded with. Of course, some white folks would rather ride extra to go to town than trade at an Indian store, but there were enough Indians and white people who didn't mind dealing with Indians to give the Sweetwaters plenty of trading.

I knew Leaf was proud of her brother, too. Cobb was a head taller than any of the other men around, even though he was younger. Something about the way he stood made you feel his strength, his calmness. Leaf's grandmother made me feel the same way. She had a peacefulness that went straight down to her toes. Sometimes I felt that stillness in Leaf, too. Maybe it came from being Cherokee, or maybe it was something special about Leaf's family. I didn't really know.

On our way into the store, we walked past two Cherokee men standing right outside the open wooden door. They wore turbans over their long hair, and loose tunics and leggings. One of the men was reading the Cherokee paper, *The Phoenix*. Leaf had read to me from the paper before. She was excited that some of the Cherokee chiefs had gone to Washington, D.C., to see the president. She had shown me the story, but I couldn't read the Cherokee words. Mama would be embarrassed to tell it, but I could hardly read any English words, let alone Cherokee ones. I didn't know why Leaf was so excited, anyway.

Washington, D.C., sounded so far away it was hard to imagine. I was lucky to get to town twice a year and that was a day away from our farm. Getting to Washington would take weeks.

I smiled at the Cherokees. I knew one of the men, Rattler. I'd seen him several times when I'd visited Leaf. He was long and thin, like a snake. He used to tease me about my heavy shoes. But today he scowled at me.

"It seems strange to see the men here today. It's not even Saturday," I whispered to Leaf. "Shouldn't they be hunting or working their farms?"

Leaf shrugged. "Too many men have been hanging around the store lately. They talk badly and are so angry. It makes me think something is going to happen. Like the eagle tried to tell us."

"I don't like the way those men looked at me," I told Leaf. "You'd think I was some varmint."

Leaf giggled. "You are—an Allie varmint," she teased.

"Then that makes you a Leafy varmint," I shot back, and glanced around the trading post. It always amazed me how many things fit inside the store. Everything from piece goods for making dresses to saddles and farm tools lined the walls. Every inch bulged with something to sell: coffee, tea, salt, spices, eggs, salted meat and fish, raisins, cheese, and even precious cane sugar. It all looked good to me. Seemed as if everything we ate had to be hog or something Mama made out of the corn Papa grew, like hominy. My mouth watered to think of all the wonderful things Leaf could eat whenever she wanted.

My favorite part of the whole store had to be the big jars loaded with taffy, fudge, and pralines. I loved lifting the wooden lids and sniffing the smooth white taffy. The sweet smell made my mouth water. Taffy and pralines smelled even better than honeysuckle.

"Allie, *tsi-lu-gi*," Leaf's grandmother called, and closed the spigot on the vinegar barrel. "You have grown prettier since I saw you last. And wetter!"

I smiled and hugged Elisi. She had powdery, sweet-smelling skin and a calmness in her dark eyes. Even at her old age, Elisi was beautiful. Her silver braids wound in a crown on top of her head. Tiny laugh lines sur-rounded her eyes, while her long red skirt and white apron hung gracefully on her slim hips. I loved that she let me call her Elisi, the Cherokee word for grand-mother. She seemed more like my real grandmother than my own faraway ones. She was always happy to see me and always ready to hug me. I couldn't remem-ber the last time Mama or Papa had hugged me.

Elisi had a way of looking at me that made me feel she really cared. She held me away from her and asked, "How is your family?"

"Mama's been tired a lot lately and Papa's been busy getting the corn in," I told her.

Elisi Sweetwater nodded. "You help your mama. We want a healthy baby. Why, the last *usdiga* I held was my Leaf. Oh, so many summers ago."

"After Mama has it, I'll bring it visiting," I said, twisting my damp hair around my finger.

Leaf handed her grandmother the plants and roots she had collected. "Good," Elisi said, giving Leaf a kiss on her forehead. "Would my girls like some taffy? I have some old pieces I was going to feed the cow." Elisi winked, reached into one of the big glass jars that sat on the store's huge wooden counter, and gave us each a long pull of taffy.

"Thanks," I said, grabbing one, "we're always glad to help you out." Whenever I visited, Elisi managed to find a treat for us.

The Cherokee men entered the trading post and Rattler spoke harshly. "You going to help your customers?"

"Hold on there, Rattler." Elisi held up her hand. "I have to take care of my precious girls."

"Nothing precious about a white girl," Rattler growled.

"You'll watch your tongue or leave my store," Elisi said.

Rattler said something to the other man in Cherokee, which I didn't understand. Leaf's grandmother snapped back in Cherokee and then the men were quiet.

"Come outside with me to eat our candy," Leaf said softly. She didn't smile. She looked so serious it startled me.

The two men watched us go out the door. Rattler spat tobacco juice on the floor right beside my bare feet. I jumped. Rattler had joked with me in the past. I wondered what had made him be so mean.

"What did they say to Elisi?" I whispered. "Why did they look at me that way?"

"It doesn't matter." Leaf shook her head. "Elisi says they need a good hunt to keep them from being so ornery."

"They gave me the shivers." I sat down on the porch steps and stuffed taffy into my mouth.

"Nobody's been doing much hunting lately," Leaf said, licking her candy. "Even Cobb is home a lot. There are councils every night. The men fuss about some white man's law."

"What law?" I asked.

Leaf shook her head. "No one would tell me. But I read *The Phoenix*. And I heard Cobb and some men talking last night about a law having to do with us Cherokees and your president."

"When Rattler and his friend leave the post I want to ask Elisi about the army. Those men in the woods were scary."

"They are like the men in the store," Leaf told me. "Lots of big talk. Besides, if you tell Elisi what happened, she won't let me go into the woods for weeks. If you're smart, you won't tell your parents, either."

I sighed. Leaf was right. I hated being cooped up at home with nothing but chores to keep me company. "All right," I told her, "but you'd better be careful." It scared me to think what would happen to Leaf if she came face-to-face with those men.

"Don't worry," Leaf said. "Everything will be fine."

I folded my sticky hands in my lap and kicked the dust with my bare toe. The front of the trading post faced the thick green woods, where the sweet smell of honeysuckle hung heavy in the afternoon heat, but behind me I could hear angry talk from the two Cherokee men. Their sound made the sugary taste in my mouth turn sour.

Wild Indian

The sun through the trees made splotches of white on my dusty legs and feet as I walked home, swinging my heavy brown shoes by their laces. I looked out over the sloped fields of our farm, but I didn't see Papa's red head anywhere. I didn't really expect to. The corn stood six feet high and would have just about covered him. Our farm might be small, but Papa always said the rich river soil made up for what we lacked in acreage. And our corn grew tall and strong in 1838.

"Allie MacAllister!" Mama yelled when she saw me coming. "Get over here right now or I'll take a switch to you!"

I sped down the dirt path with my hair streaming

behind me. I forgot all about putting my shoes on. When Mama talked switches I knew she was serious. I reached our clearing faster than a coon can climb a tree.

Mama stood on the porch, holding a rag. Sweat spotted her brown gingham dress and the few wisps of hair that had escaped her tight bun were stuck to her forehead. "Allie, you're a mess," she scolded. "Where have you been?"

"Playing in the woods," I said, hoping Mama wouldn't notice my bare feet. Of course, she did.

"Allie Marie! If I've told you once, I've told you a thousand times, wear those shoes and your bonnet. You're getting as brown as your dog."

"Yes, ma'am," I said.

"And playing in the woods, that's no place for a young lady to be. I've been calling you for the better part of an hour. There's chickens to be tended and water to be fetched, and I need you to do it." Mama rubbed her swelling stomach.

"I'll get the water right away," I said, grabbing the bucket off the porch and feeling bad that Mama had had to yell at me to help. I should do more on my own. I promised myself to help Mama all I could with the work around the cabin and not give her anything else to yell about.

"For heaven's sakes, clean yourself up while you're down there," Mama scolded. "You want people thinking you're a wild Indian?"

"Yes, ma'am. I mean no, ma'am." I sighed. After tossing a little feed to the chickens, I walked to the trees that hid the little spring where we got our drinking water. Old Jim, our hound dog, followed me to get a drink.

"You don't care if I'm dirty, do you?" I asked Old Jim as he rolled in the moss by the spring. I poured water over my feet and wiped them dry with a clump of moss. Mama wouldn't want me to get the inside of my shoes wet.

"Mama wouldn't believe me if I told her that Leaf takes a bath every morning, even in the winter," I told Old Jim. "Once a week is good enough for most people."

Of course, I hadn't believed it either. I'd figured Leaf was teasing me. So early one frosty morning I went to spy on her. Sure enough, Leaf and her grandmother stood in the river without a stitch on. It gave me goose-flesh watching them in the icy water. Brrr.

I twirled a strand of long hair around my finger and looked at my reflection in the cool, green water. I'd never be as pretty as Leaf or her grandmother. My dark hair was nice enough, but my nose stuck out just like Papa's, much too big to make me pretty. Maybe someday the rest of my face would catch up with my nose.

I dipped the bucket into the spring, figuring I better stop dawdling before Mama started fussing again.

I didn't hear Mama, though. I heard a sound that made me freeze in terror. *"Ayyyy!"* tore through the trees from the cabin.

I knew that sound. Leaf and I had sometimes practiced it on the safety of our rock, just for fun. Cobb had showed us how to do it like for real. It was a Cherokee war cry.

"*Ayyyy!*" I heard it again, and it wasn't Leaf acting silly. It was a real war cry. Old Jim barked and took off. I dropped the bucket and ran after him.

4

Trouble Brewing

It was as if the world had exploded in front of our house. I could see only dust. Then through the dust two Cherokee men appeared, galloping their horses around and around, whooping and waving rifles over their heads. Old Jim chased the horses, angrily barking as if he were chasing the devil.

I came up on the side of the house and found Mama crumpled on the porch with Papa's old rifle in her lap. I didn't think about the war cries and the dust. I was too afraid for Mama. I ran to the porch and threw myself down beside her. "Are you all right?" I called above the yells and thundering horses' hooves.

Mama looked up at me with her pale blue eyes. She was trembling all over.

"Oh, Mama, what happened? Did they hurt you?"

Mama shook her head but said nothing. I couldn't stand to see her so scared.

"Don't worry, I'll run them off," I said, grabbing the rifle. After all, Papa had taught me to shoot.

I stood on our porch and shot into the air. The Cherokees reined in their horses and looked at me. Old Jim didn't stop, though. He leaped up at one of the men and tried to bite his leg. But the man was too quick and gave my dog a good kick. Old Jim flew to the ground with a thud.

"Come here, boy," I called. Old Jim came whimpering to my side. He growled at the Cherokees, the hair standing up on the back of his neck.

"Get off our land," I snarled.

The men laughed and got off their horses. They pointed their rifles directly at me. It was pretty clear that they weren't afraid.

I don't know what would have happened next, but Mama snatched the rifle back. "Get in the house," she told me in a strong voice, even though she was still sitting on the porch and her face looked pale.

I didn't want to leave her, but I'd been taught to mind. I started backing toward the door. Old Jim stood his ground and moved next to Mama, growling something fierce.

23

The men stepped closer and Mama readied the rifle. "I'll use this if I have to," she said. Before I could tell if the Cherokees were going to heed her, another rider came into the clearing. It was Cobb Sweetwater. He shouted angrily at the men in Cherokee. I recognized only one word he said, *oginalii*. Leaf had taught me that word. It meant "friend." Cobb said it and pointed right at me.

The men yelled something back to Cobb. Then, without another word, they got on their horses and rode away.

"Sorry for the trouble, Mrs. MacAllister," Cobb said from atop Dover, his shining brown mare. "My friends are angry at the government, but they shouldn't be taking it out on you. Still, it'd be best to keep your gun handy till all this mess settles down, what with you being so close to the territory." Cobb nodded at us and rode away.

All was eerily quiet, and Mama tried to make light. "I guess they were angry about the removal," she whispered. "They've got a right to be mad, but I've got to rest now. Help me to bed."

"Yes, ma'am," I said, putting my arm around her back. I wanted to know what this removal was all about and why the men had picked on us. We had never done anything to the Cherokees. It had to have something to do with the law Leaf had mentioned, but I couldn't ask about it now. When Mama got to her feet, I saw blood on the back of her dress.

"They did hurt you!" Tears welled in my eyes.

"They didn't touch me, but they sure scared me. I felt weak all of a sudden." Mama shook her head. "I have such a hard time carrying babies. We were lucky to get you."

I swallowed hard, helping her into the tall feather bed. Leaning the rifle against the wall, I pulled extra quilts from our big, black leather trunk. They were still stained pink from the last baby's delivery.

Using the little water left in the basin, I wrung out a rag to put on Mama's forehead. She must've seen the frightened look on my face because she said, "I'll be all right. You go on now and fetch the water. I suspect you left the bucket down at the spring." She tried to smile but winced instead.

"I'll get Papa from the field," I said. He would know what to do.

"No," Mama said firmly. "Don't go getting him upset. I'll be better after I rest. Go on now, let me sleep. And, Allie, put on your shoes."

I smiled in spite of my worry. "Yes, ma'am," I said. I ran back to the spring as fast as I could, and grabbed my shoes and a full water bucket.

It was hard not to spill the water. I worried that one of those men might jump out from behind a tree. If they came back and found me, they might do more than yell. The trees around our cabin had never seemed scary before, but now I saw shadows everywhere. Leaf must

have felt the same when those white men almost found us in the woods.

When I got back home, Mama lay still on the bed, her face drained of color. I had to be quiet while I swept our floor for the second time that day.

Mama was so proud of our wooden floor. For years we'd had a dirt floor. Then two years earlier, for Mama's birthday, Papa had surprised her by nailing down the plank floor while we were out picking berries. Mama's eyes had brimmed with tears when we got home; a princess couldn't have smiled bigger. Papa had hummed a tune and twirled Mama around the cabin to try out the floor. How they had danced! Mama's dark hair and Papa's red had blurred together as they spun around. I had clapped and sung and danced beside them.

After I swept, I made sure the rest of our cabin was tidy. Everything was in its place. Onions and peppers were drying in the rafters. The cooking pot hung beside the big open fireplace, ready for supper. The sawhorse table we had brought from South Carolina sat in the middle of our keeping room, and Mama's dry sink sat off to the side. I wiped the sink and table even though they didn't look dirty.

Finally I couldn't think of anything else to do. So I went into Mama's room and sat on the floor beside her bed, rubbing my hand over the patchwork quilt she had made. I didn't think I'd ever get my stitches so small. Mama moaned softly.

I soaked a rag in water and gently laid it on Mama's forehead. Her skin was so hot! Without meaning to, I jerked back, making her stir. I had to cool her off—I knew that from other times there had been sickness in our cabin. For a long while I traded rags on Mama's forehead, always trying to keep a cool one on her.

There had been a lot of sickness in our house. The hardest time had been after Hannah died. Mama's other babies had died within a few hours of being born. I never knew them, but Hannah was different. I'd fed her. Changed her wet diaper. Washed her tiny red curls. Played with her. She'd laughed when I made her a doll.

Papa had called me the best sister ever. He said his girls were the best things in the world. With us, he didn't need the sun—we were his sunshine. He took Hannah and me on long walks in the woods. Mama used to laugh at us for taking a baby for a walk, but Papa said you were never too young to learn to love the land.

We met Leaf on one of those walks. At first she had followed at a distance. Papa saw her before I did. He whispered to me, "There's an Indian behind us." It had chilled me to the bone. I had seen Indians in town before, but they always stayed away from us. And I'd heard lots of stories about Indians at Sunday meetings when we gathered with our neighbors. Scary stories.

But there was nothing scary about Leaf. She was my size, with hair blacker than a moonless night. She'd smiled at me and I'd smiled back. We saw her on our next walk, and the next. She always smiled but never

27

spoke. Then one day I motioned to her to come closer and she did. Before long she was walking with us, holding my hand and singing loud Scottish folk songs while Hannah bounced on Papa's wide shoulders. Papa said it was like having three rays of sunshine.

That was when Hannah was ten months old. She was so much fun. But the sickness came quick and ended those happy days. One minute Hannah was laughing and trying to ride Old Jim's broad back, and the next minute she was shivering in Mama's arms. We tried to keep her cool with wet rags, but it didn't work. In two days a fever took the only sister I'd ever known.

Papa didn't say a word when he buried Hannah with her little doll. He stood by her grave for a long time as if he wanted to say something. But he didn't. I guess he just couldn't. Finally I saw a tear fall onto his cheek. He brushed it away, then went into the field to work.

Papa never talked about Hannah again. And we never went singing into the woods again, although I wanted to. I missed my papa the way he used to be. I wanted to be a family like that again. After Hannah died, the sun didn't seem to shine for Papa so much. He didn't sing. He didn't hug. He just closed up.

Mama and I cried for three days straight after Hannah died, and then Mama got the fever. There wasn't time for me to cry then, just time to work and be scared that Mama would die too. The way I was scared now.

Mama's forehead was still burning hot. The cool rags

hadn't helped. I ran to the spring for more water and tried to figure out what to do.

When I got back to the cabin, I heard moaning. Loud moaning. I dropped the bucket on the porch and ran into the bedroom. Mama was still sleeping and feverish. She thrashed about the bed. I tried to calm her by rubbing her hair the way she did mine when I felt poorly. I put another wet rag on her forehead and went outside to the porch to sit and think.

Mama had told me not to get Papa, and I didn't want to be bad, but she looked awful sick. I hugged my knees and shuddered. So much sickness and dying.

Leaf's mama had died when Leaf was only three, and her papa before that, from the measles. Leaf told me she didn't remember anything about her parents. She never cried when she talked about them. It wasn't the Cherokee way to cry, but I knew Leaf missed knowing them. At least she had her grandmother to hug her and love her.

If something happened to Mama, I'd just have Papa. Not that I didn't love him—I did. But since Hannah died Papa didn't have time for me. He only had time to work in the fields from sunup to sundown, even on Sundays. Even though Mama scolded me, she talked to me too, and explained things and made me feel important.

Old Jim walked up to me on the cabin steps and licked my hand. "What should I do, boy? Mama looks awful sick." Old Jim whimpered and I hugged him.

29

Then I heard Mama again, more like a scream than a moan. I'd never heard her sound like that before. And suddenly I knew what I had to do. Leaf had once told me that Elisi used roots to help sick people.

I had promised Mama not to bother Papa, but I could go to Elisi. "Take care of Mama," I told Old Jim, and then I ran.

I took every shortcut, even through Lacey's Stream, which was more like a snake-infested swamp. But I went through the water so fast I didn't give the water moccasins a chance to bite.

Mama could be dying. Maybe she had fallen out of bed and was calling for me. What if she died, thinking I had left her? What if she died because I had waited too long to go for help? I darted between two cedar trees and jumped over a log. Mama needed help. That was all I could think about right then.

"Ow!" My foot landed sideways and I tumbled to the ground. A sharp pain tore through my ankle. "No!" I shouted. "I've got to hurry. Mama needs me!" But when I stood up, my leg gave way. I landed on the log. "I've got to help Mama!" I began crawling. Rocks tore at my fingers and knees as I inched along. Tears filled my eyes because now I knew it would take me all afternoon to reach help. Luckily, help found me.

"Allie," Leaf said, staring down at me, "are you pretending to be a wild boar?"

I wasn't in the mood for Leaf's jokes, but I was glad

to see her. "Help me!" I cried, looking up at her. "I'm hurt and Mama's sick."

Leaf stopped smiling and pulled me up. With my arm around her shoulder, I hopped all the way to the store.

"Elisi," I yelled when we burst into the store. "Please help!"

Elisi caught me up in her arms. "What is it?" she asked.

I fought back the sobs. "Mama's bleeding and she's burning with fever."

"Is your papa there?" Elisi asked, smoothing back my hair.

I shook my head. "Mama said not to get him. But she's so sick and she's moaning something awful." By now tears covered my face and more were falling. I didn't care if Elisi thought I was a baby to cry. I just wanted her help.

Elisi calmly shooed the store's only customer out the wooden door while grabbing her leather pouch from its peg on the wall. Leaf wound my ankle tightly in a rag. Then she helped me follow Elisi out of the store and into the woods.

My ankle felt a little better, but even with Leaf's help, I could barely keep up with Elisi. Her bare feet moved quickly under her long red skirt. I knew Mama would be in good hands soon. Many people came to the store for Elisi's help.

We walked in silence, even when we crossed the

swamp. Elisi pointed to a snake upstream and we quickly scrambled onto the bank. It seemed to take forever to walk through the woods. Finally we came to the clearing.

My hand trembled on the latch to the cabin door. As awful as they'd been, I wanted desperately to hear Mama's moans. But instead there was an empty silence. I said a prayer and opened the door.

5

The Baby

"Mama? Are you all right?"

There was no answer. The house was as quiet as the graveyard. In the dim light of the bedroom, Mama lay motionless on the bed. Blood had soaked bright red spots on the old quilts.

"Mama!" I grabbed her shoulders and shook. "Please wake up!"

Elisi pulled me away and touched Mama's limp hand. "Leaf," she said, "take Allie and build up the fire. Then go strip some birch bark and find some moss."

Leaf nodded and pulled me out of the bedroom. I shook all over. It felt as if a huge tree had fallen on my chest. "Is . . . Is she dead?" I managed to ask.

Leaf shook her head. "No, she is alive or we would not need the bark and moss. Elisi will do everything she can."

"I hope it's enough," I said, wiping the tears from my eyes. "I don't know what I'd do without Mama."

"You would be strong," Leaf said firmly. "You would be strong," she repeated. "Now, come."

I didn't want to leave Mama again, but I didn't know what else to do. So I helped Leaf carry in firewood, then showed her the moss by the spring. We each carried a skirtful back up to the cabin.

In the woods Leaf found the tree she wanted. She used her knife to cut five long strips of bark.

"What does Elisi want with bark?" I asked.

"We will chop it up," Leaf told me, "and make a tea."

I shook my head. "I don't think Mama is in the mood for tea."

"It is like medicine, silly," Leaf said. "The tea helps with cramping and pain."

"Oh." I nodded and ran for a fresh bucket of water while Leaf brought the bark. I didn't say anything while we made the tea, but all the time I worried. What if Elisi couldn't help? Maybe I should have gone for Papa. He'd never forgive me if something happened.

I started praying as I'd never prayed before. I stirred the tea and begged for God's help. For Mama. For the baby.

God must've looked down on our little cabin and had

mercy, because when I took the tea to Mama, her face had some color.

"Is she all right?" I whispered.

Elisi took me into the other room. "She has lost a lot of blood. But she should be fine if she takes care of herself."

A horrible thought filled my mind. I hated to ask, but I had to know. "What about the baby?"

"The baby is fine." Elisi put her strong arms around me and pulled me close. "But she still could lose it. You and your papa must help her rest." Snuggled in her strong, powdery-smelling arms, I felt safe. I wanted to stay there. But Elisi pulled away and patted my head. "You must be strong," she told me. "She needs you."

"Papa will be home soon," I told her, trying to be brave although I didn't feel that way at all.

Elisi held my hand between her two strong brown ones. I noticed that spots of red clung to her white apron. "Your mama is asleep," she said. "Let her rest. And make her a drink of my tea every day." Then she and Leaf walked down the steps. They were already in the woods before I thought about thanking them.

When they disappeared behind some maple trees, the sun barely lit the sky. I hugged myself to ward off the evening chill. The cold kept me awake. I was plenty tired from everything that had happened. I wanted to sleep too, but Papa would be home soon. I had just enough time to warm some cornmeal mush for his supper.

I was waiting on the steps when he walked up.

"Hello, Allie, my girl!"

"Papa!" I threw my arms around his big shoulders. "Mama!" was all I could say.

Papa pushed me aside and bolted into the cabin with his boots still on. Through the open bedroom door I saw him kneeling beside the bed, holding Mama's small hand in his. I heard him talking softly to her. Mama was still asleep, so he pulled a quilt up under her chin, then quietly closed the door.

Papa looked the way he had when Hannah had died. "Is the baby all right?" he asked.

"The baby is fine," I rushed to tell him. "Mama just needs lots of rest."

Papa rubbed his forehead with his big, rough hand and pushed back a lock of red hair. "I told her she's been working too hard. What happened?"

I ladled up two heaping plates of mush and set them on the table with some hard biscuits left from breakfast. I should have been helping Mama more—then maybe none of this would have happened. If she hadn't had to yell for me to come home . . . If I had been there when the Cherokees had come, maybe they wouldn't have scared her so. So many ifs.

"I was down at the spring when I heard shouting," I whispered. "I rushed back and Mama was lying on the porch. Some Cherokees were acting crazy, riding around the yard on their horses."

"They might have killed her! Tom Eldridge warned me that something was up with the Indians and I didn't listen." Papa threw another log on the fire. He threw it so hard, sparks flew onto the hearth. "Why didn't you come get me?"

I choked back a sob. I couldn't stand for Papa to be mad at me. "Mama told me not to. She didn't want to worry you."

Papa looked at me and said in a quieter voice, "It was a good thing you were here to help. But next time you see a stranger or your mama gets to feeling poorly, come get me."

"Yes, Papa," I whispered.

Papa rolled up his sleeves and poured water into the basin. As he washed his face and hands, I was glad I'd remembered to fill the pitcher. Seems like I'd hauled enough water to fill an entire well that day, but if it'd save Mama I would've carried twice as much.

"We have to help your mama, Allie. She's delicate," Papa said, wiping his hands on a rag. I nodded. Papa and I were the tough ones in the family. We hardly ever got sick. Mama was the one we had to worry about.

I pulled Papa's boots off and set them by the door the way I did every night, taking care to wipe the mud off the toes and the floor. Mama never liked muddy boots on her wooden floor.

"Leaf's grandmother saved Mama's life," I told him when we sat down at the table. "I ran to get her since Mama told me not to bother you. If she hadn't come, Mama might have died."

Papa held up his hand. "I'll take her some roasting ears when I get the crop in." He ate the warm mush slowly, then looked at me as if he was trying to decide whether he should tell me something.

"I guess you might as well know," he finally said. "Some fool found gold in the Cherokee territory, and people are crazy to get at it and at the good farmland the Cherokees have. There's talk of trouble, and throwing the Indians out. I don't want you getting mixed up in it. Our farm and the Eldridges' are the closest to the Cherokee territory. We're easy targets for Indians mad about the trouble."

"Trouble?" I asked.

Papa nodded and wiped his mouth on his hand. "Government trouble. The Cherokees have been fighting it in the courts for years, but it's about to catch up with them. There's bad times ahead for the Indians. You stay clear of that store and your friend."

"But . . ." How could Papa ask me to stay away from my only friend?

"No buts. You do as I say," Papa said, pointing his wooden spoon at me. "Besides, Mama will need you to do all the cooking and the washing." Then his voice softened and he rubbed my head. "We want to get you a baby brother, don't we?"

38

"Papa, I promise I'll help Mama. But please let me see Leaf," I begged. Papa liked Leaf almost as much as I did. He traded at the Sweetwater store and laughed with Elisi and Cobb. How could he just abandon them like this?

But Papa was firm. "I'll hear no more about it. You do as I say unless you want a switching."

"Yes, sir." I nodded. Papa hardly ever talked switching, so I knew he was serious. But I couldn't imagine not seeing Leaf.

His hand still on my head, Papa spoke so softly I had to strain to hear him. "I've never had anything against Indians—most of them are good enough. The Sweetwaters are fine folks. But I don't want anything to happen to you. You and your mama are all I have."

I nodded again, not sure what to say. Papa usually didn't talk sweet like that. I moved to clear the dishes, limping just a bit on my sore ankle. Papa must have noticed my hobble because he helped me take the plates to Mama's sink.

In a voice I could barely hear, Papa said, "Allie, you're my sunshine." Without another word he went into the bedroom.

Papa hadn't called me his sunshine since Hannah had died. I was stunned. After I cleaned up the supper dishes, I went out to the barn and polished Papa's saddle. I rubbed on it until my arms ached and it got too dark to see. I wanted to please Papa more than anything. But I didn't understand why he had told me to stay away from Leaf. I knew he wasn't doing it to be mean, but it sure seemed that way. After all, we lived deep in the woods of Georgia, and Leaf was my only friend. Why in the world would the government care if Leaf and I were best friends?

6

Dark Land

The next day I cooked, cleaned, swept, and washed. I fetched fresh water for Mama and brought food to her bed. I warmed up Elisi's special tea and helped Mama sit up so she could drink it. I brushed Mama's hair and put it up the way she liked. I didn't have time to think about my sore ankle. It felt a little better anyway.

Toward afternoon Mama's face had more color, so I went down to the spring to fill the water bucket. I was so happy Papa had called me his sunshine and Mama was feeling better that I sang "Coming Through the Rye" at the top of my lungs the way I used to do with Papa.

41

"Hello, singing rock," Leaf said from behind me.

"Land sakes!" I yelled, brushing spilled water from my dress. "You scared the feathers off me!"

"You are the loudest bird I have ever heard," Leaf said, giggling.

"The tiredest, too." I sighed. "But all the hard work is helping. Mama's looking a lot better."

"Good," Leaf said. "It was scary to see her so sick."

"I thought you were never scared," I teased.

"Sometimes I am," Leaf said.

"You never act like it," I said.

Leaf shrugged and reached down to help me carry the bucket. I pulled the bucket away and shook my head. Leaf looked hurt and I felt bad, but I remembered what Papa had said.

"Papa told me to stay away from you for a while," I said bluntly, not knowing how else to say it.

"Why?" Leaf asked.

"He said there's some kind of government trouble."

"He means the move," Leaf explained. "I just read about it in *The Phoenix*. It's something called the Indian Removal Act."

"What's that?" I asked.

"It's a law to make Cherokees move west, to the Dark Land," Leaf told me. "Cobb said they're already giving some of the People's land away."

A strange feeling settled in my stomach. "Will you have to move?" I asked softly.

"Don't worry," Leaf said. "The law was passed a long time ago. We do not really have to go."

I grabbed Leaf's arm. "I don't want you to go anywhere. You belong here with me. You're my friend." I couldn't imagine not ever seeing her again.

"Elisi says they are just talking big, like men do. We are staying here. After all, this is our home. It always has been."

I squeezed her arm tighter. "But what if it's not just talk?"

Leaf put her hand on my shoulder and smiled. "If they try to take me away, I will splash them with water."

"I mean it," I told her, "what if the army really comes?"

Leaf stopped smiling. "I will fight them."

I could tell Leaf was serious. That made me even more afraid.

"I'd better get home now," I said. "Mama needs me. I'm sorry, *oginalii*."

Leaf touched my shoulder. "I am sorry too, Allie. But you must listen to your papa. I understand."

I didn't understand, though. A piece broke off my heart as Leaf walked away. I just hoped whatever kind of trouble it was wouldn't last long.

Time seemed to stand still after I saw Leaf. I was so busy every second with Mama. At first she wouldn't eat much. Then I asked Papa to kill a chicken. I plucked it and boiled it for the broth and tender meat. Mama managed to sip some of the broth.

43

Mama still bled a little sometimes, but I scrubbed the quilts with strong lye soap until most of the red was gone. I hung them on the tree branches to dry. My hands stung from the harsh soap, but I didn't care. It was worth a little pain to get rid of those stains. They were too much of a memory. A memory of how scared I'd been of losing Mama.

By the end of the week Elisi's tea was almost gone, but it had done its work. Mama was able to sit up and tell me what needed to be done. I was grateful Mama felt better. I was starting to feel like a chicken that had been penned up for too long. And I missed Leaf.

On Friday Elisi came by with another tea mixture in a small black pot. I wasn't sure what to do after what Papa had said about staying away from the Cherokees. Should I let her in? How could I not? Elisi had saved Mama's life. She hugged me tight and I took her into Mama's bedroom.

Mama sat up in bed, stretching out her hands. "Mrs. Sweetwater, how can I ever thank you for all you've done?"

"You would do the same." Elisi smiled and held up the pot. "I brought some more to help. Allie, would you get fresh water?"

I nodded and went to fetch the water. Sometimes I thought I spent half my life running to that spring. When I got back, I set the water bucket next to the fireplace and started to go into the bedroom, but stopped when I heard what they were talking about.

"My great sadness was my son's dying," Elisi said. "Children should outlive their parents."

"I know. There's been so much death in our family," Mama said. I could hear the hurt in her voice, and suddenly I wanted to cry for Hannah, even though she'd been dead for over a year. "This baby must live.

"I will always owe you for your help," Mama continued. "Someday, somehow, I will repay your kindness. I promise."

"No need for talk like that. You get well and send Allie if you need me." Elisi came out of the bedroom and mixed the tea.

"Is Leaf well?" I asked. I wondered if Elisi had any idea how much I missed Leaf.

"Leaf and I keep you in our thoughts," Elisi said. "Be strong. Your mother will be well soon and I am sure you will be able to see Leaf again soon too." She gave me a sweet-smelling hug and disappeared into the woods.

Neither Mama nor I mentioned to Papa that Leaf's grandmother had visited. No sense causing trouble. There was something else I didn't tell Papa. Or Mama either.

Every morning after Papa left for the fields, I would find a loaf of warm corn bread in a basket by our door. I knew Leaf left it. And I knew she missed me as much as I missed her. It was the Cherokee way to help without

45

expecting thanks. Leaf was not the kind of friend to forget you when you needed help. If I needed anything, she'd be there for me. I wanted to be that kind of friend for her, but it seemed as if I was always the one needing help. I didn't know how much things would change.

7

My Chance

Early the next Sunday morning, Mama struggled to get out of bed and dressed to go to the church meeting. "It's not very often we get a real preacher around here," she said, pulling on her woolen shawl against the morning chill. "We have a lot to be thankful for, this Lord's day."

"Maybe you should stay in bed," Papa suggested. I knew he was concerned about Mama, and I also knew he'd rather bust dirt clods than go to a church meeting.

"Nonsense," Mama said. "Thanks to Allie's nursing, I'm fit as a fiddle."

Papa sighed and went outside to hitch up the wagon. I

47

had to smile because sitting all day at a church meeting wasn't my favorite thing either, but at least I could get away. After an hour or so, I could ask to go to the outhouse and then sneak away for a while. It was something most all of the parents let their children do, as long as they were quiet about it. No one would mind, except, of course, the other children who had to stay.

"Let's have a look at you, missy." Mama tied the bow on my blue bonnet. "You look like a big sister to me," she said as she patted her stomach. "I think you'll have a brother soon."

"Brother?" I asked. "How can you tell it'll be a boy?" All Mama's other babies had been girls.

Mama winked and pulled her bonnet over her tightly bunned hair. "It's just a feeling I have. And Mrs. Sweetwater said the baby sits like a boy. I think your papa will be happy."

"Do you think he wishes I were a boy?" I asked.

Mama tied her bow firmly under her chin. "No, honey. Your papa wouldn't trade you for a hundred boys."

That was what Mama said, but I had my doubts. If Papa had a boy he'd take him fishing and hunting. They'd work the fields together and Papa wouldn't have to work so hard. I'd bet Papa would even see his way clear to get his son a horse and teach him to ride, something I'd love to do. As many times as I'd polished Papa's saddle, I'd never once gotten to ride on it. I figured if Mama had a boy, Papa'd start singing again.

Lots more people came to the prayer meeting than usual. Some I'd never seen before. A couple of soldiers and a few new families were mingling with more familiar faces in the barnyard when we drove up. Children were playing in the yard, trying not to get dirty.

A girl with a big white bow in her blond hair came up to me after I'd climbed down from our wagon. "Hello. My name is Miranda," she said. "What's yours?"

I opened my mouth to answer her, but Miranda kept talking. "We just moved from South Carolina. We had a store there. Papa is looking for a good piece of Indian land and he has his eye on a place near the river. Papa says I'll have my very own room pretty soon. I'll be glad when everything is settled. Have you been here long?"

I nodded. I'd never heard anybody talk so much at one time without even taking a breath.

Miranda kept right on. "Papa said it's about time they opened up the Indian land. Have you ever seen an Indian? I think I'll faint if I see one. Papa says he'll shoot any Indian he sees. His brother was killed by Indians. You sure don't talk much, do you?" Luckily, the bell rang to start the meeting so I didn't have to say anything.

"See you later." Miranda waved and went off to join her family. "I'm sure we'll be great friends."

I was sure I'd never be friends with Miranda, I

thought as I watched her walk into the barn with a tall, thin man, a big, round woman, and three tall boys.

The service started right after Papa and I had settled Mama into a seat. I tucked a quilt all around her to keep out the chill. We sat near the back in case she felt dizzy and had to leave in the middle of the service. But Mama seemed to be in high spirits and looked better than she had in a long time. I guessed all that rest had done her good.

We sat on a wooden plank bench for what seemed like hours. The traveling preacher hollered about sinning and slammed his fist on the wobbly table at the front of the barn. He sure seemed mad about something. Maybe he didn't like the smell. Mr. Eldridge always cleared the animals out of his barn when the preacher came around, and Mrs. Eldridge cleaned it as best she could. But the smell of animal dung still hung in the air.

I tried to listen to what the preacher said. "We are all created in the Lord God's image. We are his lambs. Let us pray together."

Everyone in the barn recited together the Twenty-third Psalm. "The Lord is my shepherd; I shall not want. He maketh me to lie down in green pastures . . ." I prayed along with Mama, Papa, Miranda, and everyone else but I wondered if the preacher included the Cherokees when he said we were all his lambs. Then we sang Mama's favorite hymn, "Amazing Grace." I was kind of hoping the preacher might be tired of talking. He wasn't, though. He started right in again. I tried to listen, I really did, but the plank benches were awful hard and a fly kept buzzing around my head.

Finally I leaned over to Papa and whispered, "May I go to the outhouse?" Papa nodded. With my eyes lowered, I eased out the heavy wooden door into a few minutes of freedom.

I really did need to use the outhouse. Even in there I could still hear the preacher. He was getting full of the Holy Spirit. "Sin no more!" he shouted. "Remember the commandments!" I hoped God wouldn't mind if I took a little break from the service.

I slipped into the woods behind the outhouse and headed for the Sweetwater store. It would be all right to go there. After all, two whole weeks had passed since Papa had told me to stay away. The trouble hadn't even happened.

I was sure Papa hadn't meant for me to stay away forever. And besides, just a quick visit surely wouldn't hurt. Mama didn't need my help right then, and the Eldridges lived about the same distance as we did from the Sweetwaters. They never told me as much, but I knew Mama and Papa had long ago figured out that a trip to the outhouse meant a play break, and they wouldn't expect me to come right back. If I hurried, Papa wouldn't even have to know I had gone so far. I felt guilty about it, but I was burning inside to see Leaf.

I didn't get far before Miranda pounced on me.

"Hello, remember me?" she said, still not giving me time to answer. "Isn't this the most boring service you've ever been to?" Her eyes rolled around as if they were loose in her head and she giggled.

"I hope God doesn't strike me down for saying this," she said, "but that place stinks. Mama says the first thing we need to do when we get rid of the heathens is to build a church for God-fearing folks."

When Miranda said "get rid of the heathens," my ears perked up. Talk like that worried me. I had never heard someone my own age talk meanly about people they didn't even know. I guess my face must have showed it.

"My," Miranda said, "you are the most serious girl I've ever met. And quiet, too."

"I have to go," I told her, suddenly wanting to see Leaf very badly.

Miranda smiled. "I'll go with you. We'll have an adventure."

I shook my head. Miranda wouldn't like where I was going. I put my hand to my ear and lied, which I knew was a terrible thing to do on the Lord's day. "I think I heard your mama calling you," I said.

Miranda sighed and headed back toward the barn. "Don't worry, I'll be back soon. So we can get to be good friends."

I waited until Miranda was behind a tree. Then I took off to be with my one true friend.

8

Just Like Me

Sparrows sang as I ran over the shady trail. The late-morning sun was soft on the red and yellow maple leaves. I stopped for a second to watch a woodpecker tap, tap, tap on a tree, eating his breakfast of bugs. My stomach rumbled, reminding me that Mama had packed cold chicken, corn bread, and buttermilk pie for the meeting picnic. Dinner seemed so far away, but I'd make it back in plenty of time to eat.

I was close to Leaf's store when I heard loud, angry voices. They scared me, so I slipped behind a large maple tree to see what was going on. I saw six Indian men standing in front of the store. Some of them had their

53

shirts off and one had red berries smeared on his chest and face. Two staggered around with bottles in their hands. Leaf's brother, Cobb, stood on the porch steps. He wore a clean white shirt and trousers. His dark hair hung long and loose.

Cobb spoke quickly in Cherokee, so I couldn't catch much of what he said. I kept hearing *dahnawa* over and over, a word I didn't know. I was ready to forget about seeing Leaf and head back to the preaching when a warm hand closed over my mouth.

My whole body froze and I squeezed my eyes shut. What was it Papa had said? "There's going to be trouble." He had warned me. Now it was too late. Trouble had just found me.

"Follow me," a familiar voice whispered into my ear. Leaf! My friend took her hand away. I was so grateful it was her and not one of the men that I giggled with relief.

Leaf squeezed my shoulder and put a finger to her lips. I nodded and quietly trailed her into the woods. I could tell from her basket of herbs that she'd been hunting for medicine plants. We made a wide circle around the store and came up to the back entrance. Slipping inside the wooden door, we padded softly up the rear steps.

In Leaf's small room the plank walls were smooth and bare, except for Cobb's painting of an eagle on one side. A heavy quilt with a log cabin design covered the bed.

It always amazed me that this whole room was all Leaf's. I had a rope bed in our keeping room, and underneath it I kept my special things in a little wooden box that had once held cigars. My hair ribbon, some pretty rocks, and the penny I'd gotten for Christmas were the only things that were mine alone. But Leaf had this whole room full of nice things to herself, with a whole big bed that she could even sit on without being fussed at.

I'd heard people talking at other church meetings. They were plenty mad that some Cherokees had better houses than them. They figured Indians didn't need houses, a hut was good enough for them. Why, to hear them talk, some Cherokees lived in mansions. Leaf's house wasn't anything like what I figured a mansion might be, but it was pretty nice.

I sank into the feather bed as Leaf closed the wooden shutters to her window. They nearly cut out the shouts of the men.

"I did not want them to see you," Leaf explained, her eyes without a hint of mischief.

"Why?" I asked, nervously twirling a strand of hair around my finger. "What's going on? And what does *dahnawa* mean?"

Leaf sat down next to me. We huddled together in the softness of her feather bed. "It means war," she said. "The men are very mad at white people. They might cause you trouble if they see you here."

"Maybe I should stay up here for a while," I whispered.

Leaf nodded. "The way some of them are drinking, they may fall down drunk pretty soon. Then you could sneak away."

"I hope you're right," I said. "I can't be gone from the church meeting too long or I'll be in deep water with Mama." With a hungry stomach, I remembered the fried chicken in the big basket. Mama would really be angry if I wasn't there to eat.

"You will be fine. Want to see the dress Elisi just made me?" Leaf asked, and opened her walnut wardrobe. Several gingham and animal skin dresses hung together, and a pair of new leather shoes sat on the bottom. Leaf pulled out a pure white buckskin dress. Small blue beads were worked into the material and more beads hung from the armholes.

"It's so beautiful," I whispered. I had only one faded brown dress to wear every day. I had to wear my petticoat at night while I rinsed it out. Mama had promised to make me a new dress after the baby came, but it wouldn't be as special as this wonderful white one.

"Why don't you try it on?" Leaf suggested. She didn't have to ask again. I threw off my bonnet, shoes, and dress. The buckskin felt like spring rain coming over my head. I'd never worn anything so soft or so pretty. I felt like a princess standing in front of Leaf's tiny mirror, admiring myself.

"I would like to give it to you," Leaf said. "In that dress you could be my *igido,* my sister."

"*Igido,*" I said with a smile. "But I can't take it," I told her. "It's too precious." I was amazed that Leaf would give me something so beautiful. But I could never take such a generous gift. Besides, if Papa saw the dress he would know I'd been to the store after he'd warned me to stay away. Papa had never actually switched me, but he'd get angry enough to consider it if he knew I'd disobeyed him.

"Elisi worked a long time on this dress, so maybe I should not give it away," Leaf said. I think she knew why I couldn't take it and how much I wanted it. "But perhaps you could wear it again when you visit."

"You're the best friend anyone ever had." I hugged Leaf and then looked in the mirror again.

Leaf picked up some of my long hair. "Let me give you braids and then you will look just like me."

I watched in the mirror as Leaf twisted my hair back and forth. With my tanned face, the buckskin dress, and dark braids I could easily pass for Leaf's sister, or at least her half sister. What would it be like to live in this nice house with all kinds of food to eat and lots of clothes to wear? I felt terrible for thinking that. I didn't mean to be ungrateful for all that Mama and Papa did for me.

At Christmas I never saw candy or an orange for Mama or Papa, but somehow there always managed to be something for me. And Mama always made me a new sunbonnet or apron from scraps she saved. I vowed not to think bad thoughts again.

"Listen," Leaf said after my hair was done. She opened the shutters and we heard only a blue jay fighting some sparrows in a nearby tree.

"They've left. I'd better hurry back to the church meeting," I said, reluctantly picking up my blue dress to change.

"We should make sure they are really gone," Leaf suggested. She started down the tiny wooden steps and I followed. I'd never noticed before how ragged my old dress was until I held it next to Leaf's beautiful new one. I almost felt jealous again, but then I remembered that this was the Sabbath and not a good day to be jealous of others. At least I had a dress.

Our bare feet fell softly on the scrubbed wooden floor of the storeroom. Leaf pulled the brown burlap curtain aside and looked inside the store. I peeked around the edge of the curtain too. There were no customers, only Elisi counting nails in a jar.

"Elisi," Leaf asked, "are the men gone?"

"Finally." Elisi nodded and gazed out the open front door. "I thought I would have to run them off myself." She paused and shook her head. "I am hungry for the old days. The time before stores, rifles, and white men."

Elisi stared off into the woods for a moment and

talked, as if to herself. "I remember the days when my sisters and I hoed corn together. We were so young and beautiful. Many young warriors wanted to mate with us, but your grandfather was the one for me. Starting this post and working hard together, those were some of my happiest days before the measles took my loved ones away."

I'd never heard Elisi speak much of her youth. I'd never wondered what it was like for her alone, without a husband. It must have been harder than she ever said.

"Is it safe for Allie?" Leaf asked. I stepped from behind the burlap and smiled.

"Oh, sweet child. Were you here listening to my ramblings the whole time? It is dangerous for you here now." Elisi hugged me and then held me away. "But this is not Allie. This is a beautiful young Cherokee maiden."

"Do you mind?" Leaf asked. "I let her try on my new dress."

I held my breath. Surely such a beautiful thing was not to be shared. But Elisi shrugged. "It is yours to do as you want. It is a good person who shares what she has. But now we need to walk with this young maiden and return her safely. No telling what a bunch of men with whiskey in them will do."

I nodded and started toward the storeroom. "I'll change quickly."

Elisi had just grabbed her shawl and pouch from the

peg beside the door when we heard shouts and horses coming fast.

"Are they back?" Leaf asked.

Elisi shook her head. "No, Cobb and the others left on foot. No good can come from whoever is in such a hurry. You two hide behind the pickle and cracker barrels." It seemed like a strange thing to do, but we minded. Leaf and I knelt together on top of my brown dress. I spread it out to protect the white buckskin dress from the floor. I pulled the bottom of the buckskin from under my legs and was horrified to discover I had pulled off one of the beads. I tucked it into my old dress. I hoped I'd be able to sew it back on before Leaf noticed.

Elisi almost had the wooden log down to lock the door when two men burst into the store, knocking her against the counter. A jar went crashing to the floor, sending pralines rolling close to my bare feet. Two more men came in through the back entrance. I recognized them. They were the same men Leaf and I had seen in the woods, Myers and Brownie. The two of them were so close I could smell the liquor on their breath.

"Where're your customers?" asked a lanky man with a stringy mustache. He was the only one of the four wearing a blue army uniform.

"They left," Elisi said, never once glancing toward our hiding place. "Is there something you need?"

Myers snorted.

"I'm sorry, ma'am." The man with the mustache silenced Myers with a glance. "I'm Captain Reynolds of the United States Army. In compliance with the Indian Removal Act, we're taking you to the new Indian territory."

9

Soldiers

"Thank you," Elisi said calmly. "But I have no plans to move."

"You have no choice," the captain said, his watery blue eyes meeting Elisi's dark ones.

A young man with a big brown hat spoke to the lanky captain. "Sir, let's grab the squaw and go," he said. "We can hit at least two other places before nightfall."

"All right, Conners. Check the rest of the house," Captain Reynolds mumbled, and walked out the door.

Myers hollered, "Take what you want and let's get out of here." In their eagerness to steal things, the men knocked bolts of material and boxes off the shelves. It sounded as if the entire store were crashing down around us. One wooden box fell right beside me, barely missing my head. I grabbed Leaf's arm, held on tight, and tried not to scream.

Conners smashed a jar with his rifle butt and scattered candy everywhere. I could smell the sweet taffy, but it turned my stomach. Conners's boot kicked into a bushel basket, sending beans the size of blueberries rolling all over the floor.

On the other side of the store, men grabbed shirts off the shelves and stuffed them into burlap bags. "Stop that!" Elisi ordered and pulled a sack away. "I am Mrs. Sweetwater and this is my store."

"You've got fine manners for a savage," one of the men yelled, and grabbed Elisi by the arm. "I'm John Myers. Pleased to make your acquaintance. But this is not your store anymore. Now, move!" He jerked Elisi's arm and pulled her out the door. Elisi fought with the man but he held her tight.

Conners snickered. "You show her, Myers."

"Stay here," Leaf ordered, pushing my hand away. I saw Leaf's small knife in her hand. She used it for cutting plants. What was she going to do with it? In a split second, Leaf lunged like a wildcat at Myers, who was holding Elisi, and sent him reeling across the front porch.

My heart pounded as I watched. If only I had a knife, maybe I could help Leaf and Elisi. I looked desperately around for something, anything, I could use as a weapon. But everything happened so quickly, there was no time. The other men poured out of the store, trying to grab Leaf. She cut Conners and Myers with her small knife before they pinned her to the ground.

Conners wrapped a dirty kerchief around his bleeding hand. "I'll teach you a little respect for white people," he yelled, raising his pistol above his head.

"No!" Elisi screamed, and threw herself in front of Leaf. The falling gun hit Elisi instead of Leaf, and she fell into the dust with a thud. She didn't move.

I think my heart stopped. Really. For a moment everything went dark and there was only Elisi slumped on the ground. Somehow I started to breathe again.

I left my hiding place and rushed to Elisi. I had to find out if she was all right. She lay still, but her eyes were open. Together Leaf and I cradled her in our arms.

"Go away!" I screamed to the men. "Why are you doing this?"

"It's the law, you wild thing," Myers spat the words at me as if I were nothing but dirt.

Captain Reynolds shot a bullet into the air. Everyone froze. He spoke harshly from atop his horse. "If you fools are finished beating up women, we can go."

Conners cussed and jumped onto his black horse. The other men mounted their horses and then Conners pointed his rifle at us. "Get moving," he growled.

"Where are you taking them?" I asked.

"You too, girlie. We're moving all you red demons out west where you won't bother decent folk again," Conners said. I couldn't believe it. They were going to move the Cherokees and they thought I was one of them.

"But she isn't a Cherokee," Leaf said.

"Shut up," Conners threatened, waving his rifle, "or this time I won't miss."

I wanted to talk, but the rifle scared me. Conners wasn't very old. He was probably younger than Cobb, but Conners was different. Conners hated and it made him seem older than anyone. When he looked at me, I could tell he hated me just because he thought I was Cherokee. His dirty blond hair and stubbly beard were normal enough. But his green eyes were different and made me feel dirty, even ashamed, even though he was the one doing bad things. I wondered if his mama had stitched his homemade shirt. Did his mama know how much he hated me, Leaf, and Elisi without even knowing us? Did she hate too?

"I can't leave my grandson," Elisi said.

"Don't worry, old lady. We'll get your grandson and bring him along soon enough. Won't be none of you people left on our land."

I shuddered at the soldier's horrible threat. But Leaf didn't seem to hear. She whispered to me as we helped Elisi off the ground. "They are taking us to the Dark Land."

I nodded and felt a chill creep over my body. The

Dark Land. The place Leaf feared. I had worried about the army taking Leaf there. Now these men were taking me, too. With Conners's rifle behind us, Myers in front, and the other men on either side we didn't have any choice but to walk.

Leaf and I took turns letting Elisi lean on us. My legs wobbled under her weight, but I wasn't about to let her fall. Dust from the horse's hooves filled the air, coating our faces and bodies. Grit filled my nose and mouth until I gagged. The midmorning sun beat down and sweat poured beneath my buckskin dress.

Dark Land. Dark Land. Dark Land. The words pounded in my head with each step I took. How could these men just take us from our home? Had the whole world gone crazy? I thought the government and the army were supposed to help people, not take them away from their families. How would Cobb find Elisi and Leaf? How would Mama and Papa know where to find me?

We left the familiar trail I knew and walked on a narrow path going west, one I'd never been on before. Trees and vines crowded the sides of the trail so we couldn't walk together. I walked in front of Elisi while Leaf came behind. Both of us were ready to help if Elisi fell. But she didn't. She walked very slowly, but she never faltered.

I fell once. I stubbed my bare toe on a sharp rock. Blood oozed from the cut, leaving little red dots on the trail behind me. It hurt. I wanted to cry, but if Elisi knew I was hurt she wouldn't let me help her, so I kept quiet in case she needed me.

It was cooler beneath the trees, but the mosquitoes found us quickly and large welts covered my arms.

"We'll never get anywhere going this slow," Conners complained.

"Keep moving," Captain Reynolds barked.

It seemed as if we walked forever on that first march. We each kept quiet, nursing our separate hurts as we trudged along.

Finally we stopped at a bend in the river. I sat on a rock and looked at my feet, scraped and crusted with dirt and dried blood. I longed for the shoes I'd left behind in Leaf's room. Mama had told me and told me to wear those shoes. I'd never again disobey her, ever. I just hoped I'd get the chance to see her again. The lovely white dress Leaf had let me wear was stained from my sweat and some of the beads had fallen off. Perhaps Elisi would be able to make it beautiful again.

Looking at the beads gave me an idea. Although I hated hurting something that Elisi had worked so hard on, I pulled a bead off and let it roll from my hand onto the ground. Maybe, just maybe, it would be a way for Papa to find me. After all, there was a bead with my old dress. If Papa found it, maybe he'd guess I was leaving him a clue. I only hoped that no one else had been in the store first and gotten rid of my dress. No, I wouldn't let myself think like that. I had to have faith that everything would be all right. After he found my old dress, maybe he would find my bead trail. Maybe. Maybe. It wasn't much of a chance, but it was all I had.

How I wished I had never put Leaf's dress on. None of this would have happened if I had still been in my faded blue dress. The soldiers would have known I was white, and they would have listened when I told them to leave Elisi alone. They would have gone to Papa and he'd have made everything all right. More than anything I wanted Papa right then. He could stop these men. He could stop this trouble. Even though he'd warned me to stay away, he would help Leaf and Elisi.

I watched while the men splashed water on their faces, taking long drinks. Then they watered their horses. The sun made the water sparkle and my mouth ached from dryness. Surely they'd let us get a drink. We couldn't walk if we died of thirst.

"Do not worry," Leaf whispered to me. "As soon as Elisi feels better, we will run off the path and find Cobb. Those soldiers could never find us in the undergrowth on horseback, and they are too lazy to walk."

Elisi had her head on her knees. Her long hands covered her face completely. She didn't look up, but we heard her whisper. "No, you must not make them angry. They will hurt you. I will continue to delay them by walking slowly."

Leaf didn't answer, but I was relieved to hear that Elisi was okay. She was walking slowly on purpose. If she delayed us enough maybe Papa or Cobb could catch up and help us. Elisi was so wise. I vowed to walk as slowly as possible too.

The captain interrupted our planning. He told us we could drink from the river. We had to go one at a time so we couldn't try to get away, he said. I went last and listened to the men talking as I gulped the cold, muddy water from my hands.

"Stupid Indian figured he could stop us. Just 'cause he owned that store, he thought he could tell a white man what to do," Conners said.

Myers laughed. "That boy won't be telling anyone what to do now. That bullet stopped his mouth for good."

I choked and looked up at Myers. He spat tobacco juice into the water and laughed.

"Shut up," Captain Reynolds told the men. Something about the captain was different from the others. He didn't hate Indians. I could tell by the way he looked at me. He didn't smile, but he looked sad.

"Let's go," Captain Reynolds ordered, and we started walking west again. I hadn't even had time to wash my bleeding toe. Elisi stumbled along. She was such a good actress that I feared she wasn't just pretending to be hurt. She seemed to really be in pain. Was it just a few days before that I hadn't been able to keep up with her?

69

How would she feel after I told her that her grandson was dead? Killed by these men?

I looked at Elisi, praying that the men had been lying. Praying that all this craziness would stop. How could God let this happen? A purple bruise the size of an apple had formed on Elisi's forehead where Conners had hit her. Leaf shadowed her grandmother, grabbing her elbow several times to keep her from falling.

The men made no effort to help. Captain Reynolds led the way and never glanced back toward us. Brownie plodded along in front of us on his bay horse. I didn't feel sorry for his horse anymore. I just felt sorry for myself, Leaf, and Elisi. Conners rode behind us on his big black horse and Myers brought up the rear on his black mule. Conners and Myers had their rifles at the ready, watching every step we took.

"This squaw is too damned slow," Conners complained again.

"You're the one that hit her," Captain Reynolds said. "Keep moving."

We walked along the river until we came to a cabin. "This is the Eastmans' place," Leaf whispered. "Don't worry, they'll help us." I was so grateful. All I wanted at that moment was a place to rest.

Leaf threw back her long hair and glared at Myers. She looked so certain that our troubles were at an end, I felt a glimmer of hope.

Myers snickered and readied his rifle. "Let's go get us some more Indians."

"Watch them," Captain Reynolds ordered Conners. The captain and his men rushed into the cabin. I wanted to call out and warn the Eastman family inside, but Conners had his rifle pointing at me. I knew one peep out of me and he'd hit me. Besides, it was too late—the men were already inside.

Leaf and I huddled on the ground close to Elisi. "I'm sorry you were dragged into our troubles, Allie," Elisi whispered to me. "Your papa will come soon to take you home."

I bowed my head so I didn't have to look at the ugly swelling on her forehead. "He won't worry until evening," I whispered. Mama would be angry that I missed dinner, but they wouldn't be concerned until it was time to go home. By then, there was no telling how far we might have walked. Silently I pulled another bead off my dress and let it fall to the ground.

"Do not worry," Leaf said softly. "Cobb will find our trail. They have not even tried to cover our tracks."

I didn't say anything, but I knew Cobb wouldn't be following us. I had an awful feeling that the men had told the truth and Cobb Sweetwater lay dead somewhere in the woods behind us. I couldn't bring myself to tell my friend that.

10

Half-Breed

"Shut up," Conners hollered. "Stop all that whispering." He sat chewing a long piece of straw and pointing his rifle at Elisi.

Elisi sat up straight, putting her hand on my shoulder. "I must tell you this child is not a Cherokee."

Conners looked at me and spat out a piece of straw. "Looks like a half-breed to me," he grunted before turning to look at the cabin. The screams from inside the small log house made me shiver.

Elisi squeezed my shoulder and tried again. "She is a white friend of my granddaughter."

Conners didn't even bother looking at me this time.

"White girls don't wear outfits like that," he said. "They aren't that brown, neither. And they don't make friends with your kind."

I looked down at my buckskin dress and remembered Mama's words: "You're getting as brown as your dog." I wished I had worn my bonnet more, the way Mama always wanted me to. And hadn't Leaf said, "In that dress you could be my sister"? Why hadn't I changed? My blue dress still lay crumpled behind the pickle barrel.

I swallowed hard and spoke up. "You can't do this to us. My papa will never stand for it."

"You'll see your papa soon enough," Conners said, repositioning his rifle toward my face. "We're rounding up all the breeds. Georgia's sick of your kind."

"But he isn't—" I started.

"I'm not arguing with a little snit of a squaw," Conners snapped. "If you ain't Indian yourself you're friends with them and that's good enough for me. Shut your mouth or you'll be sorry."

I didn't say anything else. I just watched while the other men pulled an Indian man and woman and two boys out of the Eastmans' cabin. The man was bare-chested, with strong muscles. He looked furious, ready to fight. The woman talked to him in Cherokee and pulled on his arm. She was Mama's age and with child. It looked as if she was begging him not to fight. After the man answered her in Cherokee, he turned from the soldiers and called to the boys. They were a little older than me and bare-chested too.

The boys stepped to their father's side and waited. It was hard to watch what Conners and Myers did. They punched the father in the stomach and ordered him into line with us. Then they ordered the boys and their mother to follow.

When the Eastman family walked by me, I could see into their eyes. The mother and younger son had tears in their eyes. The father and older son had a look like Conners had. It was a look of hate. But none of them made a sound. Captain Reynolds yelled, "Let's move," and we all started walking.

We followed a trail covered with pine needles that constantly pricked my bare feet. The Eastman family didn't speak to us and we didn't have a chance to talk to them because the soldiers made us walk in silence. We walked for hours until I thought I couldn't go one more step. Then we stopped at another cabin. I dropped another bead off my dress. Thankfully, I still had plenty left for my trail.

"This is the Wellses' place," Leaf confided to me. "They are so old, I don't think they could walk very far."

I stared at the little cabin. It had a red rosebush blooming beside the porch. What would Conners and Myers do to people who couldn't walk?

Captain Reynolds took the men inside just as he had

before and left Conners to guard us. But this time the captain and his men came out quickly.

"They're gone," Captain Reynolds called. "Let's move."

"They left supper on the table," the tall man named Myers said. "They knew we were coming." As we walked away, I saw Myers set fire to the cabin. I could smell the smoke as we moved deeper into the woods. The smoke wasn't so bad, but Myers's laughter brought a lump to my throat. Somewhere nearby, I was sure, the owners of the house were hiding and watching. They had no choice but to look on helplessly while everything they owned burned. If they were too old to walk, how could they live without their house? I truly hoped they couldn't hear Myers's laughter.

I was sorry then that I had gulped down so much water. I tried to ignore it, but the pressure got worse and worse. I wanted to run behind a tree to relieve myself. How I wished for the Eldridges' outhouse. It would seem like a palace. I would sit patiently through days of preaching if I could just go back to that barn again.

I looked back at Brownie. He was chewing tobacco and slouching on his bay horse, his rifle propped across the saddle horn. Maybe he wouldn't mind if I ran off a ways behind a tree to relieve myself. I waved my hand and asked, "Can I go behind the tree for a minute?"

Brownie laughed and I could see the tobacco juice in his mouth. "Not on your life," he said with a laugh, and raised his rifle in my direction. I started to argue, but I could tell it was hopeless. I concentrated on holding my bladder until I felt sick to my stomach. Finally I could hold it no more. Warm water rolled down, stinging my dusty legs and leaving streaks on them. Before long I noticed that Leaf and the others had done the same. I was embarrassed for all of us. Leaf, who bathed every morning, was now filthy.

But she didn't complain and neither did I. It wouldn't have done any good. Besides, Brownie, Conners, and Myers would have enjoyed our misery.

▼▼▼

Our group walked through the daylight and into the setting sun. Had it been only that morning that I was safe with my parents at the prayer service? So much had happened, I felt like a different person. Shadows from the woods made me think wild animals were watching us. I was scared. Every once in a while an owl would hoot or a wolf would howl. Even Conners acted frightened by the sounds.

It always cooled off in our part of Georgia on fall evenings, and the breeze felt light and comforting on my cheek. But the setting sun didn't help my feet any. The bottoms of my feet burned as if hot coals lined the path instead of dirt and dried pine needles. The dried blood had formed a crust on my toe, and it still throbbed. I was glad to stop at the next cabin, although I knew it meant more prisoners. I needed rest, even with Conners's rifle pointing at me. I knew Elisi needed the break as much as I did. I had given up on the idea that she was pretending. She walked slowly because she had to, although a part of me still hoped she was fine. Leaf didn't tell me who lived in the cabin. Maybe she didn't know. Maybe it didn't matter anymore. She just sat and stared at the ground, her long hair covering her face. She didn't look up when we heard fighting and screaming.

I started to ask Leaf if she was all right, but everything got very quiet. From our place outside on the ground I saw Captain Reynolds take two small boys and a woman older than Elisi out of the cabin. The little boys clung to the woman's skirt. Next a screaming woman kicked Brownie as he pulled her out the door. The woman held a baby in one arm, and she fought off Brownie with the other. Brownie threw the woman and the baby into the dirt. Then the whole front porch exploded with fighting. Myers rolled out the door, struggling with an Indian man. He punched the man while Brownie kicked him over and over.

"That's not fair," I shouted. "He's outnumbered."

"Too bad," Conners said with a grin.

Captain Reynolds stepped on the porch as the Indian dropped to the ground. Blood was splattered all over the Cherokee's blue shirt. I thought he was dead, but he groaned when Myers kicked his side.

"We'll sleep here tonight," the captain said with a

stone face. Then he shook his head, turned, and went back inside the cabin.

Conners sat on the porch, his rifle aimed toward us. The other men went inside, leaving the hurt Indian where he had fallen. His wife huddled beside him. Before long the smell of frying bacon filled the air. I was so hungry, the smell made my stomach ache. But no one offered us anything, not even when Brownie replaced Conners on the porch. Brownie didn't make a sound unless someone groaned. Then he chuckled.

"What kind of man enjoys someone else's suffering?" Leaf whispered to me. I didn't know.

We sat in the dirt, staring at the cabin as night fell. I knew that back at Mr. Eldridge's, church services were over and Mama and Papa were looking everywhere for me. First they'd be mad, then they'd be scared. Mama might even cry. I didn't want her getting worried. It was dangerous for the baby. It didn't matter how much I fretted; there was nothing I could do about it, except pull another bead off my dress and drop it on the hard-packed ground.

The night grew cold. Elisi pulled her woolen shawl around us as we all lay down. Beside us the other prisoners huddled together to sleep. The two little boys' voices echoed in the night breeze before their grandmother quieted them in Cherokee.

"They want to know why they cannot sleep in their own beds," Leaf told me. I wondered the same thing as the baby began to cry.

"The poor child is cold." Elisi sighed and pulled her shawl away. Immediately the night air swept over me. Leaf and I sat up and watched Elisi hobble over to cover the woman and her baby. Silently the woman shared the shawl with her hurt husband. Elisi paused for a moment in the starlight, then pulled something from the leather pouch around her neck. She knelt down beside the man for several minutes.

I lay back on the cold ground, looking at the stars. Mama and Papa were home now, looking up at the same stars, wondering where I was. For all they knew, I had run off or gotten eaten by a cougar. Maybe they wouldn't look for me. After all, the baby was due and Papa couldn't leave Mama and the farm. Maybe I had made Mama so upset that the baby had come early and it was a boy, as Papa had always hoped. Then they wouldn't need me anymore, especially when I had caused so much trouble. I would have done a hundred chores without even being asked if I could just be safe at home again. A tear slid down my cheek, making me colder than the night air ever could.

When Elisi came back, she sat between Leaf and me and tucked us under her big, heavy skirt. "Snuggle together," she said. We scrunched up tight. Being close to Elisi made me feel as if someone was watching over me. I felt her shiver and I realized that Elisi was cold too. I tried to think of some way to help her, but I was so tired I fell asleep.

Sometime early the next morning, while it was still

very dark, I woke up. Someone moved. It was Captain Reynolds. I held my breath as he stood beside the little boys, the moon casting just enough light for me to see them all. The captain took the blanket from his shoulders and laid it over the tiny sleeping figures. Then he quietly went into the house. Myers grunted from the porch where he sat keeping watch.

I burrowed my head back inside Elisi's skirt and fell asleep again until the dawn exploded with rifle shots.

11

Morning Fire

Elisi squeezed Leaf and me close as two shots boomed through the morning silence. She held us so tightly we couldn't move. I didn't open my eyes even when I felt the sun warm my cold cheeks. I was afraid to see what had happened. I hoped those shots meant help had come, that someone had taken Conners, Brownie, and those other horrible men far away from us. But I was afraid they did not mean that.

"Get up!" Conners yelled from the porch. I opened my eyes as Elisi pulled her skirt away and the cold morning air rushed over me. I hugged myself to keep warm. The others did the same. None of the Indians had

81

proper warm clothing. Only the two little boys had a blanket.

Brownie carried a few sticks of firewood and some kindling from the porch. He dropped them in the dirt, then went inside the cabin and came out with a burning twig, which he used to light a small fire.

"What in blazes are you doing?" Conners bellowed at Myers.

"Captain said to make these Indians a morning fire," Myers spat back.

Conners shook his head and raised his rifle toward us. "Not too close," he warned. "No tricks."

Nine of us gathered around that tiny fire, which most days I could have put out with my spit. But that morning I didn't have any spit. Thirsty and hungry, I huddled as close to the warmth as I dared with Conners watching. I listened to the others speak in Cherokee and felt alone.

I caught a few words that Leaf had taught me. *Sv-no-yi* meant night. *Ti-s-qua-lv-da* meant run. The rest I couldn't understand, except for boy, *a-tsu-tsa*. When the old woman motioned to a boy sprawled on the ground at the edge of our makeshift camp I understood. The Eastmans, the first family we had picked up, were gone. They must have gotten away during the night, except for one of their sons. That was what the gunfire had been about that morning. One son had been shot and his family had been forced to leave him behind. Maybe they hadn't even known he'd been shot and were still hoping he'd catch up.

"We could have gotten away too," Leaf whispered to me. "We could have been free."

"Or we could be like him," I said, nodding toward the boy who couldn't have been more than thirteen. The shoulder of his shirt was stained bright red. Elisi left the fire and carefully knelt beside him. She pulled his shirt away and Leaf went to help her. Elisi gave the boy something from the pouch around her neck and Leaf used Elisi's apron to wrap his shoulder. The boy nodded his thanks.

I hated to leave the fire but felt as if I should help. Before I had the chance Conners yelled at me, "Tell them to get back from the fire."

I looked at Conners and shrugged. "Get back from the fire," I said to the old woman and her family. They looked at me with blank eyes and I knew they didn't understand me.

Conners was beside me and snarled, "Tell them in Cherokee, you fool!"

"I don't know how," I explained. "I'm not a Cherokee."

"I won't play that game with you, girl," he snarled. Then Conners kicked me in the leg, knocking me to the ground, and aimed his rifle butt at my chest.

Before he could strike, a wagon pulled into the clearing, brimming with furniture, supplies, and children.

Conners left me sprawled on the ground and went back up to his chair on the porch. A white man and woman stepped down off the wagon and entered the cabin. The children stayed in the wagon, peering over the edge at us. Something about them reminded me of Miranda, the girl I'd met at the church meeting, a lifetime ago it seemed then.

"Are you all right?" Leaf asked as she helped me off the ground.

I rubbed my leg. It was sore but not broken. "I'm fine, but I wonder what they're doing here," I said, nodding to the children in the wagon. "They act like we're going to scalp them."

"Maybe we should," Leaf said. I looked at her, expecting to see a teasing smile, but her mouth was a hard line.

In a few minutes Captain Reynolds came out of the cabin. "Let's move," he ordered. Rifles were aimed at us as horses were saddled and the walk began again. The Indian man who'd been beaten leaned on his wife. The grandmother carried the baby while the two boys held on to her skirt. Elisi told me the family's name was Bridge. The wounded Eastman boy staggered along by himself. He wouldn't let anyone help him.

As we moved away from the clearing the white family began carrying things from their wagon into the cabin. The children clambered down from the wagon and one of the older boys stuck out his tongue at us.

"How can they do that?" I asked Leaf and Elisi. "That's not their house. How can they just move in like that?"

Elisi and Leaf didn't answer. But I knew they were thinking the same thing I was. Someone was moving into the trading post.

Then I remembered Miranda saying her papa wanted a place by the river. My stomach churned. Elisi's store was near the river.

12

Rain

West. We always moved west. We walked in silence, too troubled by what we were leaving behind to fear the Dark Land that lay ahead.

"Remember the time Cobb took us hunting?" Leaf whispered, interrupting my thoughts.

I had to smile. Cobb had spent days helping us make tiny bows with arrows. Then we'd walked into the woods like regular hunters. Of course, we hadn't caught anything, but that didn't matter because Cobb had showed us so many things about the woods.

"Never eat this plant," Cobb had pointed out. "It will kill you overnight." I looked along the trail, hoping to see the plant. If I could get the men to eat the plant our troubles would be over. I didn't really want to kill the men, but it didn't matter because I didn't see the plant.

I did see Leaf watching the sky, and that reminded me of something else Cobb had taught us, how to find our way by the sun. That was how I knew we were traveling west, into the land of Leaf's nightmares.

"Cobb will find us," Leaf said to me.

I nodded with a big lump in my throat. I wanted to tell Leaf the truth. I knew Cobb wasn't coming. But I couldn't say those words to my best friend.

Two days of walking with little water and no food had made my legs feel like fence posts. I had never been so tired. I tried to keep my mind off the terrible journey. I thought about the only other long trip I'd ever taken when my family traveled from South Carolina to our new Georgia home, just outside the Indian territory. In South Carolina Papa had shared Mama's family's farm, hoping someday to save enough to buy his own. But when Papa's brother died and left him the Georgia land, Papa couldn't wait to move. He was excited about his new farm, but Mama was sad about leaving Grandma and Grandpa behind.

It had been a long, miserable journey. I had thought it would never end. I was only five, but I still remembered how awful it had been. But this was much worse. At least then I could ride in the wagon when I got tired.

Sometimes I had even slept on the bouncing wagon seat, leaning against Mama. I had no one to lean against now.

Elisi walked slowly but steadily, never complaining. I was certain she wasn't pretending anymore. She was really hurt. The Eastman boy who'd been shot staggered along, and I wondered if his parents were watching us, waiting for their chance to help him. If they were, they must have suffered to see him struggle so. Maybe they were nowhere near us. Maybe they had no choice but to leave him behind to go to the Dark Land with us.

We were all struggling, thinking of those we had left behind, hoping they would rescue us. I knew Cobb could not come, and the boy's family had no strength against this small army. Would Papa be as helpless? Maybe I was foolish to think he could save us.

The Bridge family seemed the weakest. The baby cried almost constantly and the two little boys whimpered, clinging to their grandmother and making it hard for her to walk. But the worst sound was the grandmother's wails, the most pitiful, chilling noise I'd ever heard. I was almost glad when Conners yelled, "Shut up or I'll shoot the bunch of you!" I don't think they needed to know English to understand his threat.

Leaf must have felt sorry for the little boys because she scooped them up and carried one in each arm. I was so tired I didn't know how Leaf had the strength, but I also knew I couldn't let her carry them alone. I took a little boy of about three. He smiled at me with sparkling brown eyes, played with some of the beads on my dress for a while, then fell fast asleep on my shoulder, sucking his thumb.

At first it was pleasant to hear him sucking away and to feel his warm body close to mine. Before long, though, my shoulder felt as if it would break under his weight and my right arm went numb. I tried putting him on my left shoulder, and that helped for a while, until that arm lost its feeling too.

Then the rain came. It fell lightly at first and cooled our bodies, sticky from the afternoon heat. I held out my tongue to catch some water.

As the trail became steeper, the skies ripped open and dropped streams of water on our heads. Tiny, muddy rivers formed around our feet, and the dense, driving rain made seeing difficult. I worried that our trail would be washed away, along with my beads. Desperately I tore another bead off and dropped it in the mud beside me.

"Oh, no," I moaned when I stumbled over a rock and almost dropped the little boy. "Can things get worse? Rain is all we need."

"Maybe it is." Leaf stooped to help me up on the narrow tree-lined trail. "In this mess we should be able to slip away easily."

I looked down the embankment beside us. There was

no way a horse could follow us there. The men would have to chase us on foot.

"But what about Elisi?" I asked. "Is she up to it?"

Leaf nodded, then flung the rain off her face. Conners shouted and we started walking again.

"Give your child to his *elisi*," Leaf commanded. I obeyed and felt guilty that the little ones had to walk again. It gave me chills to think about leaving them behind.

I worried as I watched Leaf hold Elisi's arm. Could we do it? Could we get away? Or would we end up shot, like the boy? Or worse? Elisi shook her head several times. I could hear only a little of what Leaf said because of the storm, but I knew she was telling Elisi that we should make a break for it.

"It is our chance to get away," Leaf said.

Elisi shook her head. "It is too dangerous. I do not want you to get hurt."

Leaf kept talking and talking. I heard her say, "I do not want to go to the Dark Land." Thunder rumbled in the distance and my heart beat so that I thought it would jump out of my chest. If Elisi agreed, what would happen? Even if we did get away, would they chase us forever? If we found our way home would they take us again? Leaf and Elisi might not even have a home anymore.

Leaf must have been persuasive, because finally Elisi nodded her head. Leaf turned. Our eyes met. *Now!* Leaf said to me without words. A second later the three of us ran between the trees. Weeds whipped our legs, and rocks tore our feet as we hurtled down the slope. We had almost reached a deep ravine when shots rang out. Elisi fell to the rain-soaked ground.

"No!" Leaf screamed and fell beside her. Blood oozed from Elisi's thigh and Leaf quickly pressed her hand to the wound. I froze, staring at the blood. How could this be happening?

"Keep going," Elisi begged. "I will be all right." I looked at the ravine and the hundreds of hiding places it afforded. They would never find us there. I looked at Leaf and I knew. We couldn't leave without Elisi. Kneeling down in the pouring rain, I lifted Elisi's head out of the mud. Blood dripped from between Leaf's fingers and spilled onto the ground.

Leaf pushed me. "Go, Allie. You are not even Cherokee. Run!"

"No!" I shouted. "I won't leave you!"

"Hurry," Elisi urged, "before it is too late."

But it was already too late. Conners approached on foot, pointing his rifle. "Stupid Indians! Get your carcasses back on the trail!" he bellowed and shoved his warm gun into my back.

"She's hurt," I called over the rain.

"You! You shot her!" Leaf screamed, and jumped at him with bloody hands. I grabbed Leaf's arms and held her away from Conners. I didn't want her shot too.

"I should shoot you all," Conners yelled. "It'd save me a lot of trouble."

I held Leaf tight until I felt her stop struggling. When I let go she dropped down beside Elisi.

Conners spat tobacco juice at Leaf. "Damned Indians," he snapped. "You shouldn't have run! It's your own fault!"

13

Village on Wheels

"Why did you shoot her?" Captain Reynolds asked, towering over us as we huddled on the ground around Elisi. His black boots were almost touching Leaf's mud-covered knees.

"They were running away," Conners growled.

Reynolds shook his head. "She could barely keep up before, and now she'll have to ride. Put her on your horse," he ordered.

Conners stared in disbelief. "My horse?" he said.

"That's right," Reynolds said, his face a hard mask.

"I ain't putting that animal on my horse!" Conners roared.

For a long moment Reynolds stared at Conners. Finally the captain said, "I'll not have our progress slowed because you were eager to shoot." Without another word, he walked off to his horse and the line of Indians.

Conners lifted his rifle. For a horrible second, I thought he might shoot the captain in the back. Instead Conners jerked Elisi off the ground, then half dragged, half carried her up the slope. Everyone in our group could hear his cussing as he slung her onto his black horse.

Elisi winced but never said a word about the bloody spot on her thigh. The old Mrs. Bridge hurriedly wrapped Elisi's leg with a strip of underskirt. The white material quickly turned bright red.

"Move on!" Captain Reynolds yelled, and Conners jerked the reins on his horse to jolt Elisi along. The trail widened enough for Leaf and me to walk on each side of the horse, holding on to the stirrups for support in the mud. I leaned against the horse's black belly, smelled its wet hair, and felt the warmth of its body. As the rain continued to pour, that heat gave me strength to keep going.

The creaking of the leather saddle took my mind back to the first time I had surprised Papa by polishing his old saddle. I had worked at night until it had shone like a cat's eyes in the dark. Papa had whistled when he'd seen his old saddle shined up the next morning. "Allie, you're my official saddle polisher from now on," he'd said.

"Do you really like it?" I'd asked.

Papa had nodded and patted my head. "I sure do. It wouldn't look half so pretty if I'd done it myself," he'd said.

I gulped. Papa would have to polish his own saddle again without me unless I could find a way home. I pulled another bead from my dress and let it fall into the mud.

Lightning flashed overhead as we came to a clearing surrounded by sycamore trees. "Gather them up," Captain Reynolds shouted. We clustered in a circle with the men's rifles aimed at us. I was becoming so used to having guns pointed at me that I barely realized they meant danger. The rain was coming down so hard I was surprised to see Elisi looking into the sky. I looked too, but I didn't see anything.

Without a word, Leaf suddenly bolted from our group and ran to the trees. "No!" I screamed when Conners raised his rifle. Suddenly I remembered what a gun could do. I lunged toward him and pulled the barrel down.

Conners slapped me across the face and sent me reeling into Elisi's horse. I didn't care; I didn't want him to shoot Leaf. Elisi's blood still stained the front of Conners's shirt. I didn't want Leaf's blood there too. Maybe I'd given her time to get away. Maybe she was going for help. But I couldn't believe Leaf would leave us.

Leaf didn't get far, though. Myers grabbed her up by

the waist and threw her at me. "Keep your butt with the others," he yelled.

"Are you crazy?" I yelled over the storm as I helped her off the muddy ground. "Do you want to get killed?"

"I needed this to help Elisi's wound." Leaf held up a strip of bark. She popped it into her mouth and chewed. Brown juice ran down her chin.

"That's horrible," I told her. "I'm hungry too, but I wouldn't eat that."

"It is not to eat," Leaf said. She eased the softened bark under Elisi's bandage. Elisi looked down from Conners's horse and nodded at Leaf.

"Damn, these stupid Indians and now this all-fired rain," Conners muttered. "Aren't we ever going to see sunshine?"

I looked at Conners and lifted my head. I was Papa's sunshine. He needed me. I dropped another bead. Home with all the chores was the only place I wanted to be right then. Home. Sunshine. I kept saying those words over and over in my mind.

Although the sun didn't shine, the rain eventually let up a little. Through it all we kept walking west. Elisi rode with her head up and never said a word, even when an occasional gust of wind sent rain in strong sheets.

The rain fell like needles, pricking my skin in thousands of places. I bent my face down to stare at the mud, to keep my eyes safe from the stinging rain. Mud, horses' hoofprints, and more mud were all I saw. The rhythm lulled me and I was half asleep when Leaf whispered in my ear, "I know this trail. They are taking us to the Cherokee village."

I had never seen the village before, but Leaf had talked about it often. Elisi had grown up there, and Leaf's father had been born there. The Sweetwaters visited the village once a year for the Green Corn Dance. Leaf had told me about the many people who gathered, laughing, telling stories, feasting, and dancing. Hundreds of Cherokees still lived there, although many had moved away to start their own farms or run businesses, like Elisi.

Leaf grabbed my shoulder. "We will be safe there. Indians will be everywhere. The soldiers will surely be defeated."

I wanted to sing. We were going to be all right. These foolish men didn't know what they were doing. We would be safe as soon as the Cherokee braves captured them.

Leaf must have felt the same because she actually did sing. " 'Amazing Grace! How sweet the sound.' "

The men were so startled they didn't stop her, and I joined in with Leaf. " 'That saved a wretch like me! I once was lost, but now am found.' "

It felt so good to sing with Leaf again. For a moment we were happy. But then a strong burning smell filled the air and Elisi moaned, "Oh, no. *Tsi-sa.*" She had called on Jesus for help. If something was wrong up ahead, I prayed that he would hear her.

No one, not even Conners, uttered a word as we came upon the village. Even the little boys fell silent.

No singing. No parties. No feasting. No braves waiting to pounce on our captors. Not a single child or dog ran freely in the village. Most of the homes were smoldering ashes in the rain. Strewn around in the mud lay smashed clay pots and ripped clothing. We walked past a dead dog. It had been shot in the stomach. Immediately I thought of Old Jim, grateful he was safe at home.

"What have they done?" Leaf moaned. "Even the council house is gone." We walked to the center of the village, where a few stubborn flames licked the roof of a huge building. The smell of burning wood hung over us like death. The hell the traveling preachers yelled about must look like this.

Everywhere there were wagons. And they were filled with Cherokees, guarded by white men with rifles.

"Here." Captain Reynolds stopped and pointed. Conners quickly pulled Elisi off his horse and pushed her toward an open wagon.

"Get in." Conners motioned with his rifle. One by one, we climbed into the wagon bed. Leaf and I helped Elisi get up. Inside, three children huddled beside one woman wearing a torn dress. Two older women stood up and helped Elisi sit down. They spoke to her and Leaf in hushed tones. I couldn't understand them. I sat beside Leaf and looked at the two Indian men in the wagon. Big, rusty chains bound their feet and hands. Conners wasted no time chaining the men from our group, even the injured Eastman boy. I felt sorry for him. He looked so pale and worn that I feared he wouldn't make it much longer.

"Spread out and help the others," Captain Reynolds ordered his men. "Make sure everyone is out of the village. Myers, watch these Indians."

Myers started to complain but spat tobacco into the mud instead. Conners whooped and headed into the nearest house that wasn't burning, a small plastered abode with a thatched roof. In a few minutes he came out with a long red-and-blue beaded belt, which he stuck into his saddlebag.

"They're stealing!" I cried to Leaf. How could he do that right in front of us? I wanted to take that belt and hit Conners with it. I looked at Leaf. Her eyes filled with hate. Then I remembered the way the men had stolen from the store.

"My moccasins!" one of the small children cried. The mother quickly quieted him. One of the Indian men in our wagon tried to stand when he saw Conners walking around with his son's moccasins, but Myers shoved his rifle into the man's chest and pushed him back down with a warning. "Sit or I'll shoot." We all knew he meant it.

I sat on the pine floor of the wagon for a long time

without saying a word. The smoke from the burning houses stung my nose and eyes. My beautiful white dress was brown with dirt and sweat and heavy with rainwater. I pulled several of the beads Elisi had so lovingly sewn and scattered them on the ground beside the wagon. Twisting a strand of hair around a dirty finger, I tried to catch some rainwater in my mouth. My lips cracked when I opened them, they were so dry. I wanted my papa and my mama. At twelve, I knew I was too old to be such a baby, but I couldn't help it.

Every once in a while someone whispered something to Elisi or Leaf in Cherokee, but no one spoke to me. I couldn't even understand their words. The soldiers might think I was Cherokee, but no one else was fooled. I was not family. I had never been to the village. I did not belong there. I jumped when Leaf leaned toward me and whispered, "Do not worry. The army will figure out their mistake and you will leave us. You will be all right."

"We'll be all right," I said firmly, looking up into the sky. "Look, the rain is stopping."

"The sky has no more tears," Leaf said. She said something else too, but I couldn't hear because the wagon jerked forward and started bouncing over the trail. Leaf and I linked arms to brace against the jolts.

The late-afternoon sun came out and quickly steamed the wagons dry. An odor of wet cotton and hot bodies hung over us. We headed west again, farther away from home. We traveled the rest of the day and into the night. I dropped beads along the side of the wagon as we moved until finally I had no more to drop. Every bead was gone.

Leaf watched the trail closely. My insides hurt too much from the constant bouncing to watch where we were going. I didn't cry out, because no one else did. But I wanted to.

At last I fell asleep on Leaf's shoulder. When I awakened the coolness of night had its icy grip upon us and we had stopped. I couldn't see much in the dark.

Conners pointed his rifle at us. "Get out!" he hollered. "This here is your home until we can get you to the territory." He meant the Dark Land.

When I stood up, everything hurt from my head down to my throbbing toe. Leaf was helping Elisi out of the wagon, so I scrambled to help too. Conners herded us into a fenced area. The first thing I noticed was a terrible smell—mud and urine, mixed with sweet honeysuckle. Huddling in a muddy corner, we heard others groaning around us in the darkness. Babies' cries mingled with coughs as I stared into the black night.

14

White Man's World

I wished for the night's darkness when I saw our prison the next morning. Rough posts had been strung together with many strands of wire to make a pen. It was the same wire Papa had used to make a chicken coop after a fox had killed three of our hens. Our prison had no roof, and mud puddles made up the floor. I couldn't tell how many pens surrounded us, but there were others and each was squeezed full of sleeping Indians.

Leaf lay beside me, staring at the sky. We stared for a long time without speaking. Clouds rolled by, unaware of the misery we were in. Nothing changed until an eagle appeared, a lone eagle soaring high above our pen. One of the guards must have seen it because he shot into the air. But the eagle flew away, unharmed.

"Something big will happen today," Leaf whispered hoarsely.

Her words made me afraid. Surely this camp was as bad as it could get. I turned toward Elisi. Her eyes were open and she was staring at me. After a few minutes, she nodded and closed her eyes. I looked around. Everywhere people huddled, seeking warmth in the chilly morning.

"I've never seen so many people all together," I whispered.

Leaf kept looking into the sky. "Cobb warned us," she whispered. "They mean to get rid of every Cherokee in Georgia. I hope he finds us soon."

"I can't believe they're doing this." I shook my head, trying not to think of Cobb being dead.

"I cannot believe they shot Elisi," Leaf said. We both looked at Elisi's still form. The bruise on her head had turned an ugly purplish green. Strands of silver hair fell across her face, partly covering the swelling. Mud clung to her wet skirt and a patch of dark brown stained the skirt covering her right leg.

The whimpers and coughs of cold children surrounded us as people awakened. No one spoke, except to soothe a child. Mud coated everything, even the trousers of the soldiers who walked outside the fence. My dress, caked with brown slime, was ruined. Not even Elisi could fix it now.

Then I had a horrible thought. How would Papa know those beads I dropped were mine? Even if he found the first one by my old dress, what would make him look for more beads? For the first time, I felt completely hopeless. How would anybody find me? Leaf must have read my thoughts because she put her hand on my shoulder.

"Cobb will come," she assured me. "Somehow he will save us." I couldn't let my friend have this useless hope. Cobb was not coming. My father was not coming. Leaf and I would be better off if we believed the truth of our terrible situation and forgot about hope. Nothing would change for us.

"Leaf," I said softly. "Cobb is dead."

Elisi moaned, but Leaf tore her hand away from me as if I were on fire. "You lie!" she yelled. "All white people lie!"

I kneeled close to Elisi as she moaned again. "I'm sorry," I said quickly. "I shouldn't have said anything. He may be fine."

"No. He is not fine. Things will never be fine again." Elisi opened her eyes and looked at the sky. "Cobb is better dead than here, covered with the white man's mud."

"Cobb is alive. Allie cannot know for sure," Leaf told her, glaring at me.

Elisi moaned as if she hadn't heard. "It is a terrible thing for a mother to outlive her children, and her children's children." Then she closed her eyes. She didn't open them for the rest of the morning, even when Leaf checked her leg.

Why hadn't I kept my mouth shut? I hated myself for making Elisi so unhappy. I hated myself because Leaf had stopped speaking to me. And I hated myself for being white.

After a morning of ignoring me, Leaf grew restless. I watched her move around our crowded pen asking the Cherokees huddled together if they knew anything about Cobb. She sat down beside an old man for a long time, while I squatted in the mud beside Elisi.

I was thinking about Mama and Papa when Elisi put her hand on my arm and whispered. "Allie."

I leaned close. "I am old now," she said, almost to herself. "As a girl I had no fear. My husband and I lived in love until he died of the white man's sickness."

Elisi grimaced in pain. I wished I knew how to help her. If only I had listened when she'd told Leaf about healing herbs, and made my own medicine pouch to help her. But I had nothing.

Elisi's eyes clouded as she went on. "I cannot help Leaf. I will soon be with my husband and son and grandson. They called me last night."

"Elisi, I don't understand. You are sick. I . . . I will find help. Everything will be all right." I looked around.

Elisi must have been crazy with pain to be talking about dead people being near.

"Don't be scared." She spoke faintly but firmly, and I knew she hadn't gone crazy. "Cobb called to me in my dreams. But I cannot leave this place until I know that Leaf will be safe. This is the white man's world. I must leave her in your care."

"Please, don't talk this way." I choked out the words.

"The Real People, my people, believed the white man's promises and treaties too many times. But this promise you must keep. I cannot rest until I know Leaf will be well."

"But they think I'm a Cherokee too," I said with tears welling in my eyes.

"This dawn, I opened my eyes," Elisi whispered. "An eagle soared over you. It was a sign. Will you help her?"

I stared at the ground, unable to speak. "Give me a hug," Elisi told me. "You are stronger than you think." I gently put my arms around Elisi and she held me close. Elisi said I was strong, but I felt like a baby who just wanted her grandmother to keep her safe.

"Promise me," Elisi whispered.

I sat back, twisting my hair and thinking. If I promised, I was telling her she could die. I didn't want that. I needed her and so did Leaf. But when she squeezed my arm I swallowed hard and whispered, "I promise."

Elisi looked into my eyes before she nodded. Then she leaned her head against the fence and closed her eyes.

15

The End

Leaf didn't say anything when she came back and I didn't ask. The truth about Cobb was better left unsaid. Elisi put her hand on Leaf's shoulder and we sat in the mud. All we could do was wait. Wait to find out what they would do to us next.

The sun beat down without mercy, and by mid-afternoon it had baked dry most of the mud on us and on the ground. For the second time in my life, I wished I had my old blue bonnet. If the guards hadn't brought some corn bread and water, I would have fainted from the heat.

While we ate our tiny portions the old Mrs. Bridge

started wailing again as she had on the trail. When a guard walked over and hollered, I figured she'd quiet down, but the guard left and she kept on. It was a miserable sound, but I knew how she felt. It was the sound of a life without hope.

A few minutes later an empty wagon drove up. Two white men came into our pen. They grabbed the hands and feet of Mr. Bridge, the Indian man who'd been beaten. Now I knew why Mrs. Bridge was wailing so loudly. Her son was dead. The two men tossed him into the wagon like a sack of flour. The old Mrs. Bridge, her daughter-in-law with the baby, and the two little boys stood at the fence until the wagon's wheels were no longer in sight. They stood, waiting and waiting. But no one came back to tell them where they'd taken the body.

As the day wore on, an old Indian man came to look at Elisi's leg. He spoke in Cherokee for a long time. Elisi answered and took the pouch from around her neck. When she opened it, I saw that it was empty.

"I should have gathered more herbs on the trail." Leaf groaned and jumped up from beside me. She grasped a fence post with her bare hands and shook it.

A guard hit the fence with the butt of his gun. "Get away from the posts," he ordered.

Leaf slumped down. The old man chanted in Cherokee until dusk. Elisi was silent long after he left. Then she motioned for Leaf to come close.

I could not hear what Elisi said, she spoke so softly. Finally she closed her eyes and Leaf turned to me. "She said I must stay with you because she is going to my father. She told me to never forget Cherokee ways." Leaf squeezed her eyes shut and held my mud-crusted hand until we fell asleep.

In the middle of the night I awakened, cold, hungry, and scared. I wanted to go home. In my misery, I started sobbing. A hand on my head startled me. It was Elisi. I know a good Cherokee doesn't show emotion, but Elisi didn't scold me. She just hugged me tight until finally my tears stopped. We found a little warmth huddled together under the great starry sky.

The last thing I remember of that night was Elisi whispering to me in a weak voice, "It will be all right, brave girl."

In the morning Elisi was dead.

I awoke first and touched her cold, stiff hand. It was Elisi, but it wasn't.

"No! Wake up," I whispered as I kneeled beside her, tears streaming down my cheeks. "I take it back. You can't die. We need you. I can't help Leaf alone. I need you."

But it didn't matter. She was gone. Gone, the person who'd always had a smile for me. Gone, the only grandmother I'd ever really known. Gone, the only person who'd always been ready to hug me. She was with her husband now, and her son, and Cobb.

I wanted to run fast and far into the woods and never

look back. But in our prison there was no place to go. When Mama was sick, Elisi had come and made everything all right. But no one could make Elisi all right. I cried so hard my insides hurt.

When Leaf awoke she didn't cry; she just held her grandmother's hand. I tried to pull Leaf away, but she shook her head. "I killed her," she said softly.

"What are you talking about?" I asked.

"If we had not run, she would not have been shot," she said. "I killed her."

"Don't be crazy," I told her. "You didn't pull the trigger. It was Conners. He did it."

"But I asked her to run." Leaf paused. "She did it for me."

"Because she loved you," I said. "Don't forget that."

Leaf nodded and we were silent. I knew Elisi's dying was my fault. I'd told her she could die. I'd promised her I would take care of Leaf. It wasn't Leaf. It was me. I had killed her.

I didn't understand how God could let so many bad things happen. My head hurt and my face was raw from the cold morning and my tears. I was so sad, I thought I would cry forever. But when I thought about how wasteful it was that Elisi had to die, hatred replaced my tears. Hatred such as I'd never felt before. I hated the soldiers who had done this to Elisi. It wasn't God's fault, it was these stupid men. It was Conners and Myers and Brownie and even Captain Reynolds. If I could have, I would have killed them with my bare hands. I stared at the ground, trying to figure out what to do.

"We have to tell the guards she's dead," I said finally.

Leaf shook her head. "No, we will say she is sick."

"Leaf, they'll know. Soon they'll be able to tell." I couldn't let Elisi just lie there in the mud, but I didn't want to see her dragged away and thrown in a wagon, either.

"I will not let them take my *elisi*," Leaf vowed, clutching her grandmother's hand. Leaf was my best friend. So I did as she asked and hoped the guards would not look too closely.

That night, sleeping beside Elisi's body, was the longest, coldest, and darkest night I had ever known. I was startled when I realized that some of the moaning I heard came from me.

The morning brought more cold rain and coughing from the prisoners. Leaf still held Elisi's hand.

I was surprised when a small white woman with gray hair appeared before us with an old, faded patchwork quilt and a green blanket. She took one look at Elisi. "Oh, honey," she said to Leaf. "What's wrong with your granny?"

"Nothing," Leaf lied. "She is not used to sleeping in the rain."

"I'm real sorry about this," the woman said. "Maybe I could arrange for her to spend the night at my house. No one as sick as your granny should have to sleep out in weather like this." She moved to put the blanket on Elisi.

Leaf quickly took the blanket. "Thank you. I will take care of her," she said.

"Oh." The woman rubbed her hands on her white apron. "If you change your mind, just ask the guard for Mrs. Rollins." The woman paused a minute and whispered. "This isn't right, I know. I'm . . . I'm sorry."

Leaf nodded her head slightly. She waited until the woman walked to the other end of the pen before wrapping Elisi in the blanket.

"Leaf," I whispered. "We should have told her everything. She was nice. Maybe she would have helped."

"I do not want white help." She spat out the words like poison.

"I'm white," I pointed out. "If we tell Mrs. Rollins our story, she may help us get out of here."

Leaf didn't say anything; she just looked at Elisi's still face in the green blanket. We sat silently for the rest of the morning. Leaf held Elisi's hand the whole time. I felt empty. My head pounded so hard, I could barely think. When Mrs. Rollins came back I would tell her the truth about everything. How I was white and Elisi was dead. How I promised to take care of my best friend. Mrs. Rollins would have to help us. Somehow I would convince Leaf to go along. I had to. I had to get Leaf out of here.

I hugged my knees and rocked to stay warm as the

rain trickled to a stop. Myers walked by, whistling a tune, and I hated him. I hated his happy song, just as surely as he hated me and Leaf and all the Cherokees. Elisi was dead because of him and his army.

Finally I could take it no more. I bolted past Elisi. Past Leaf. Past the moaning women. I couldn't go far in our pen, but I weaved around the crying babies and wounded men. I needed to find Mrs. Rollins. She would help us. I searched, but it did no good. Mrs. Rollins was gone. And so were my hopes. I sank to the muddy ground and wailed, just like old Mrs. Bridge. All my hope was gone.

Then I remembered Mrs. Rollins's words, "Just ask the guard for Mrs. Rollins."

I grabbed hold of the fence and called. "Please," I asked the guard. "Please tell Mrs. Rollins I asked for her."

The guard was a huge man much more interested in his cigar than me. He took a drag, blew out the smoke, then looked at me. "Mrs. Rollins ain't interested in the likes of you," he said.

"But, she said—" I started.

"Shut up," the guard grunted, waving his rifle at me, "and get away from the fence."

I started to argue more, to beg, but I could tell it would do no good. The guard walked away and urinated on a fence post, close to old Mrs. Bridge. I turned away in disgust.

Dragging myself back to Leaf, I tried not to cry. There would be another chance. Mrs. Rollins had come once; she would come again. She had to.

At noon Leaf cried out when an empty wagon drove up beside our pen. "They cannot take her," she said. We held tight to Elisi, burying our faces in her cold body. I couldn't bear to let them drag Elisi away from us. We heard the guards talking and opening the gate of our pen. I squinted out of the corner of my eye to see what was happening.

But when the mud-covered boots stopped in front of us, no one jerked Elisi's body from us. Leaf and I didn't breathe until the boots walked away.

There was something familiar about those boots. I looked up and saw the back of a tall red-headed man. "Have you seen my daughter?" he was asking the Eastman boy.

"Papa?" I whispered, not believing it could really be him. "Papa!"

The man turned and looked at me. "Allie?"

I flew into his arms, crying.

"Oh, Allie. I've looked everywhere. I didn't even recognize you," he said. "I passed you by."

"It's me, Papa," I cried, burying my face in his chest.

Papa rubbed my filthy hair and whispered. "I was afraid I would never find you, Sunshine. I found the little bead you left in your dress and I found a few along the way, but when a farmer told me he heard 'Amazing

Grace' from the Cherokee village I had a feeling it was you."

"I'm so sorry I didn't mind you at the prayer meeting," I sobbed.

Papa's strong hands held me close, not caring that I was covered with mud. "I can take you to your mama and baby brother now," he said softly, wiping the tears from my eyes. "Mama had the baby at the Eldridges' farm. They're just fine and waiting for you."

I stopped crying. Mama had her baby. They were all right. And Papa still loved me. He hadn't forgotten me. I was his sunshine, even with a new baby boy. Everything was going to be all right. Then I looked down. Leaf still held on to Elisi.

"I can't leave without Leaf and Elisi," I told him, choking on the words. All I wanted was to get out of that horrible place, but I couldn't leave Leaf alone.

Papa knelt beside Elisi, still wrapped in the rough green blanket. "Mrs. Sweetwater's dead," Papa said solemnly, touching her arm.

"I promised her I would help Leaf. I will not break my promise, even if I have to stay here."

Papa looked at me, then at Leaf, then at Elisi. Silently he stooped and lifted Elisi's body.

Papa carried Elisi past the old Mrs. Bridge, who had wailed for her son. Past the younger Mrs. Bridge with the baby and two boys. Past the wounded Eastman boy. Past many others I did not know. Leaf and I followed.

Every Cherokee in our pen stared at us. I couldn't bear to look at them. I was safe, but their nightmare would not end. Leaf touched Papa's arm and pulled the blanket away from Elisi.

Leaf's voice quivered when she spoke. "Elisi does not need this anymore. She would want this baby to have it." Leaf wrapped the blanket around a baby.

Leaf had done the right thing. I wished we had more blankets to share. A guard reluctantly opened the gate. *Good-bye, terrible man,* I thought. Old Mrs. Bridge started wailing again as the guard slammed the heavy wooden beam over the gate. I shivered and walked straight ahead to our wagon, not more than twenty yards away.

Papa gently lowered Elisi onto the wagon bed. He was helping Leaf and me onto the wagon when Conners grabbed his shoulder.

"Where do you think you're taking these heathens?" Conners yelled.

Papa spoke calmly. "Captain Reynolds said I could take my daughter."

"Looks to me like you've got a whole tribe. Captain never said anything about that," Conners snarled, and pointed his rifle at Leaf.

"I was wrong," Papa said. "I have two daughters here."

Conners grabbed Leaf's arm. "You're not taking this squaw anywhere."

"Let her go!" a strong voice commanded.

Conners didn't move. Captain Reynolds called from his horse a second time. "Let her go!"

"This man is taking an Indian," Conners roared.

Captain Reynolds aimed his pistol at Conners. "I gave you an order. Let her go!" Conners pushed Leaf's arm away and stormed off.

Papa climbed onto the wagon seat and saluted Captain Reynolds. Reynolds nodded and rode away.

I felt something on my mud-crusted hand and looked down. It was Leaf's hand holding mine tightly. Her other hand was in Papa's. She didn't look at me or at Papa, but a big tear slid down her face. I had never seen my brave friend cry before. But there was no shame in her tears.

I followed her stare to the pens. Hundreds of brown eyes looked out from behind the poles. Tears burned tracks down my face, and the pain in my belly was so strong, it almost broke me apart. We couldn't just leave everyone there. I heard a baby crying and looked at Papa.

He shook his head. To my surprise, tears rolled down his rough cheeks. "I'm sorry, girls," he said hoarsely. "This is the best I can do."

Leaf and I both nodded. Papa slapped the reins and together we went home.

Author's Note

When I was a little girl, I visited the Cherokee reservation in North Carolina and saw a play about the Trail of Tears. The injustice of moving an entire nation of people from their homeland merely because their skin was a different color made a powerful story that I never forgot. Later I found out that I have Cherokee blood in me. Like Will Rogers, I felt "I am part Cherokee, and it's the proudest little possession I ever hope to have." Because of sketchy records, I don't know if any of my ancestors walked the Trail of Tears, but they may have. And I feel a powerful connection to this sad story.

Most of the trouble between the Cherokees and white

settlers started because Indians lived on land that white men wanted. When gold was found in Georgia, tensions got worse. In 1830 Congress passed legislation called the Indian Removal Act, forcing all Indians, including the Cherokees, off their land. During the next several years, the United States government tried to take all Indians from their homes in the eastern United States and move them to land west of the Mississippi River.

The Supreme Court said this law was illegal, but President Andrew Jackson refused to honor the Supreme Court's decision, even though his life had once been saved by a Cherokee brave. In 1838 the Cherokees lost their legal battle to remain in their homeland. Four thousand Cherokee Indians died as they were forced to walk hundreds of miles to Oklahoma. The long, woeful trip of many months became known as the Trail of Tears.

Allie and Leaf's story is fictional, but there are truths woven into it. Not all white people who lived in the 1830s hated Indians. Many were horrified by what happened and tried to help the Indians in small ways, like Mrs. Rollins in my story. Some Cherokees did escape the Trail of Tears by hiding in the mountains. Some may even have sought refuge with white families.

I wrote this story in tribute to my grandmother Lillie Bailey. I loved her very much. Just like Leaf and Allie in my story, I will never forget my *elisi*.